Darkwood

Darkwood

M. E. BREEN

BLOOMSBURY

NEW YORK BERLIN LONDON

Published by Bloomsbury U.S.A. Children's Books
175 Fifth Avenue, New York, New York 10010

Page vii: Lines adapted from Rolfe Humphries's translation of *Metamorphoses* by Ovid

Library of Congress Cataloging-in-Publication Data
Breen, M. E.
Darkwood / by M. E. Breen.—1st U.S. ed.
        p.   cm.
Summary: A clever and fearless orphan endures increasing danger while trying
to escape from greedy, lawless men and elude the terrifying "kinderstalks"—animals
who steal children—before discovering her true destiny.
ISBN-13: 978-1-59990-259-3 • ISBN-10: 1-59990-259-1
[1. Adventure and adventurers—Fiction.   2. Orphans—Fiction.   3. Human-animal
communication—Fiction.   4. Sisters—Fiction.   5. Wolves—Fiction.   6. Fantasy.]   I. Title.
PZ7.B74822Dar 2009   [Fic]—dc22   2008044413

First U.S. Edition 2009
Book design by Donna Mark
Typeset by Westchester Book Composition
Printed in the U.S.A. by Quebecor World Fairfield
2 4 6 8 10 9 7 5 3 1

All papers used by Bloomsbury U.S.A. are natural, recyclable products
made from wood grown in well-managed forests. The manufacturing processes
conform to the environmental regulations of the country of origin.

For my mother, brave in battle

Men spread their sails to winds unknown to sailors,
The pines came down their mountain-sides, to revel
And leap in the deep waters, and the ground,
Free, once, to everyone, like air and sunshine,
Was stepped off by surveyors. The rich earth,
Good giver of all the bounty of the harvest,
Was asked for more; they dug into her vitals,
Pried out the wealth a kinder lord had hidden
In Stygian shadow, all that precious metal,
The root of evil. They found the guilt of iron,
And gold, more guilty still. And War came forth
That uses both to fight with; bloody hands
Brandished the clashing weapons. Men lived on plunder.

—Ovid, *Metamorphoses*

Darkwood

Chapter 1

The sun sets so quickly in Howland that the people who live there have no word for evening. One minute the sky is blue or cloud gray, the next minute it is black, as though someone has thrown a heavy blanket over the earth. Nowhere is the sky darker or the night longer than Dour County, a hatchet-shaped region on Howland's western border. A swift river runs through Dour County. Slippery cliffs overhang the river. An icy sea roils off the coast. But worse than these is the forest that grows to the north. No roads mark the forest and no human footprints. Like the dark, it has lives of its own.

"Nonsense! After seven centuries, you think the moon is going to show its face for you? Come away from there now and set the table."

Annie Trewitt took a small step back from the window. She had seen pictures of the moon in books, copied from older pictures in older books, copied from the oldest books of all. There were the skinny crescent moons, the half-shadow moons, the regular full moons. And then there were the Howler moons, round and orange and edible looking, even on the page.

"I told you, come away!" Aunt Prim shoved a stack of clean dishes into Annie's hands and reached past her to fasten the shutters. "If it's the kinderstalk you're peeping after they'd better be worth a whipping." She paused dramatically. "He *will* catch you one of these days."

Annie followed her aunt's gaze over to the chair where her uncle was enjoying his third nap of the day. Drool snaked in a clear line from the corner of his mouth to the collar of his shirt. Around one finger he wore a battered tin cup like a ring, a little residue of whisky at the bottom.

Annie set three bowls on the table, three spoons, and three cups. A fourth set of dishes sat on the shelf, untouched. The insides of the bowls had been scrubbed to a smooth gray finish, exactly the color of the porridge that filled them at every meal. She poured milk from an ewer into each of the cups, careful first to spoon the cream into a separate dish for her uncle's dessert.

Aunt Prim's voice sounded close at her ear. "Mind your uncle well tonight, hear me, girl?"

Annie nodded, but Aunt Prim crowded closer, her lips nearly touching Annie's cheek. She smelled of cotton, milk, and dust.

"Do you hear me, girl? Do you hear me warning you?"

"Yes, Aunt Prim, I hear you."

"And you can't say I didn't warn you, can you?"

"No, I can't say you didn't warn me."

"Swear to it, then."

Swear to it? Annie glanced sharply at her aunt. She looked herself—long and dry and pointed, like a rib bone—and also not herself. Her eyes were bright, and a little frizz of hair stood up around her face.

"Do you swear?" Aunt Prim repeated, but before Annie could swear, or pretend to swear, Uncle Jock woke up.

Waking took a long time for a man as big as Uncle Jock: first the feet twitched, then the knees, then the hands, and finally the long chin lifted off the chest. He sniffed the air.

"Come to table, dear," Aunt Prim said. "You know you don't like your supper cold."

If waking was slow, standing was slower. Annie had plenty of time to scoop porridge from the big iron cooking pot into each bowl, then add pickled vegetables and salt pork from the jars her aunt had replenished that day in the shed. Uncle Jock's bowl was twice the size of the others and Annie filled it to the brim. She heard the floorboards creak and then he was standing beside her, massive as a mountain that had torn itself up from the ground. But he was solid, not fat; he could move fast enough when he wanted.

"Jane came past today," Aunt Prim said as they took their seats. "The Woeforts' new cow was taken last night. That's not more than a stone's throw from here."

Uncle Jock grunted.

"They'd just finished the fence around the barn, too. Twelve feet high, Jane said, spiked all along the top. Not so much as a hoof left in the yard." Her eyes slid over to her husband. He was digging at something in his ear with the long dirty nail of his pinkie finger. "Something *was* left behind, however."

Uncle Jock stopped digging. Aunt Prim smiled and took up her spoon.

"Well?"

Aunt Prim nibbled her oats.

"*Well?*" Uncle Jock banged the table with his fist. Porridge slopped over the side of his bowl.

Aunt Prim leaned forward. A pulse beat at the base of her throat. "A tuft of hair."

"A tuft of . . . what color was it?"

"What *color?*"

"Yes, woman! What color?"

Aunt Prim frowned, all coyness gone. "That's odd, you know, I thought Janie must be joking when she said it, but now . . ."

"*What color!*"

"White! She said it was white."

Uncle Jock became very still. From the corner of her eye, Annie could see his lips puff in and out. After a moment he picked up his spoon and began to shovel porridge into his mouth. Annie had managed only a few bites when he pushed his empty bowl away, stretched, and let out a tremendous belch.

"Primmy my gal, I'm still as hungry as a bear."

Aunt Prim raised her eyebrows.

"And do you know what I fancy, my very own Primrose?"

Aunt Prim raised her eyebrows a notch farther.

"Haddock."

Annie's heart sank. Aunt Prim's mouth, which was long without being wide, flattened even more. But all she said was, "Girl, go down the hall and get your uncle some fish."

~⁂~

Aunt Prim stored the fish with the dry goods in a shed off the back of the house. What she called the hall was really just a pile of boards slapped together and nailed at the top into a triangular crawl space. All the farms in Dour County were built like this, the sheds and outhouses connected to the main buildings through closed walkways or tunnels. No one kept more food indoors than was needed for a single day, and those foolish enough to try raising livestock built their barns as far from the main house as possible.

Annie squatted down to unbolt the door to the passage. An ax hung over the door and she caught her reflection in the polished blade: dark eyebrows, blank face. Aunt Prim handed her a single match from the tin matchbox.

The bare ground felt cold and foreign under her palms. Even with the light spilling in from the main room, the darkness of the passage shocked her; it seemed she wasn't moving through the dark so much as being swallowed by it. Every few feet she paused, listening. It was odd, what Aunt Prim had said about the white fur. Everyone knew that kinderstalk were black. Black to match the night. She shivered. They kept a lantern in the shed, of course, but the light from the house never reached quite far enough, and Annie spent a moment in awful, fumbling darkness before she heard the match strike.

Though she hated getting there, the shed itself she liked.

The walls began a few feet below ground, which made it cool in summer and warm, or at least not frigid, in winter. Bags filled with oats sagged against each other and against bins of salt, onions, and lard. There was a barrel full of the misshapen potatoes that still grew, somehow, in the blighted yard. Thin strips of fish hung drying from the rafters, next to bunches of sage and rosemary. As the fish dried they shed scales that coated the floor in a stinking, shimmering dust.

Annie chose a big piece of fish for her uncle, then two smaller ones, wrapping them carefully in a scrap of cloth before tucking them into one of the many pockets of her dress. The dress she was wearing was two years old and ridiculously small, but Annie refused to give it up. Page had made it for her, sewing by lamplight in the swallowing darkness while Annie slept beside her. The dress had dozens of pockets: some wide and flat for long-stemmed plants, some narrow and deep for rocks or shells. There were obvious pockets, and then inside the obvious pockets there were secret ones. There were pockets in the lining of the dress that only Annie could ever get to, pockets in the armpits, pockets in the hem. The dress was so perfect for her, for her habits of observing and collecting and hiding, that at first she had hated it. How could Page know her so well? What was the point of a secret compartment if Page only had to look at her to guess what was in it? Then Page died, and Annie had worn the dress every day since.

The passage was easier to manage on the way back, with the light coming through the open door to guide her. She had almost reached the door when she heard her aunt's voice.

"Annie? Annie girl? Are you there?"

Annie hesitated. She could see the outlines of her aunt's face and the tight, small bun she wore framed by a square of orange firelight.

"Annie dear?"

The hair on Annie's arms prickled. She eased backward a few feet.

Aunt Prim chirped her name again, and then said in her regular voice, "She's still in the shed."

Uncle Jock's legs came into view, his big knees level with Aunt Prim's shoulder.

"Can't you shut the door, just to be sure?"

"Oh, Jock, come now. The fright would kill her."

He chuckled. "A little thing like the dark?"

Uncle Jock bent down and peered into the passage. Even in silhouette, Annie could make out the heavy flaps of skin that hung from his neck and jaws. His . . . what had Page called them? His *dewlaps*.

"Not a lively kind of a girl, is she? Not like the other one." Uncle Jock placed a hand on top of his wife's head and levered himself upright. "I sent word. Everything's set."

"Jock, are you sure? She's strong for her age, and like you say, not too clever. In a few years she could take over the cutting."

"It's done."

Aunt Prim put a hand to her hair, neatening the bun that Uncle Jock had squashed. Then she stood and moved out of sight. Annie crept forward, straining to hear her next words.

"I made a promise to Helen."

For a few moments all Annie heard was the squeak of the pump drawing water from the well into the sink, then the faint splashing sounds of her aunt washing her hands. When her uncle spoke again, his voice was almost . . . Annie winced. Almost tender.

"Primrose, it was only a matter of time. He's run us clean out."

"But the Drop, Jock? Such a waste."

They moved farther away then, their voices growing muffled. Annie had stopped listening in any case. The Drop. They were sending her to the Drop, and she would die there.

Every night after dinner the three of them followed the same routine. Aunt Prim ironed the laundry, Uncle Jock cleaned his rifle, and Annie scraped out the cooking pot. Normally this was a chore Annie hated, but tonight she was glad for the chance to hide her face inside the pot and think.

She'd waited another few minutes out in the passage, then, making as much noise as possible, crawled back into the room. If she hadn't been so frightened it would have amused her to see them arranged around the table just as before, her aunt polishing an invisible stain with her rag, her uncle scowling into his bowl. The rest of the meal had passed as usual, only now Annie read some secret communication into each scrape of her aunt's spoon, each wheeze of her uncle's breath. More than anything, she wanted Page to be there. Page would have known what to do.

The fire had died to embers by the time Annie's head and shoulders emerged from the pot. Uncle Jock had long since finished cleaning his rifle, and having restored it to its place by the head of the bed, had restored himself to his place by the fire and begun to snore.

Annie straightened abruptly, preparing to return the pot to its shelf. As she did, she bumped into Aunt Prim, who was crossing the room with a pile of freshly ironed breeches. The pile swayed for a moment as if deciding whether or not to fall, then toppled to the dirt floor. In an instant, Annie was on her knees.

"Get away! You'll only make them dirtier." Aunt Prim shoved Annie aside with her hip and bent to reach for a pair of breeches. As she leaned forward a small book fell out of her pocket. The two of them stared at it, then at each other. For the briefest moment it looked as if Aunt Prim was going to cry. Instead, she snatched up the book and shoved it back in her pocket, but not before Annie saw that the margins were filled with notes written in Page's tiny, precise hand.

"Out! Get out of my sight, you clumsy girl!"

Uncle Jock shifted in his chair. Aunt Prim clamped her lips together and jabbed a bony finger in the direction of the ladder that led up to Annie's garret room. Annie scurried up it, but after she had crawled into the garret and let the trap-door slam behind her, she silently opened it again, just a crack. She watched her aunt glance at her uncle, still sleeping, then cross to the bed and slip the book between the mattress and the frame.

Annie let the door down gently. She walked to the window and peered out. Her face peered back at her. In daylight she had a view of the privy roof, and beyond that a fence, a field of stumps, and finally the dark wall of trees that formed the forest's southern edge. It was bad luck to put a window facing the forest. Everyone knew that. But her father had built this part of the house, so she didn't like to think of it as a mistake.

The garret had been their parents' bedroom. A wooden cradle stood under the eaves, used first by Page and then, five years later, by Annie. And now . . . Annie reached down and lifted out the warm, limp body of an orange cat. Isadore hated to be held, but when he was asleep she could pretend for a few moments that he liked it. She sat down on the only other piece of furniture in the room, a mattress facing a row of empty shelves. Their parents had owned dozens of books on every subject: geography, agriculture, medicine, folk stories, woodworking. Some of the books were handmade, the bindings sewn together with heavy thread. Others were bound in shiny leather with gold letters stamped on the front. There was a *History of Mining* and a *Guide to Weaponry*, a bestiary and a giant dictionary with a tattered red cover. There was a grammar of ancient Frigic, a cookbook devoted to the preparation of grubs, a volume of love poetry. Page read them all. She had hurt her ankle as a baby and it never healed properly, so she scooted herself from sink to fire to ironing board on a stool with runners fastened at the ends of the legs, like a sleigh. As soon as she finished her chores each day she would make her way to the garret to read. She read her way through the volumes stacked in wobbly towers around their little room, moving each book from the unread to the read pile after she finished it. When she had finished them all, she started again from the beginning, making a new pile for books read twice, then another for books read three times, and so on. After Page died, Uncle Jock had come into the garret and taken away all of her books and clothing. "Fever," he said, and burned them along with the body.

Annie released the now wide-awake and squirming Isadore. Immediately, a brown striped cat climbed into her lap. Annie scratched her ears.

"Prudence, *you* are an excellent cat." She unwrapped a piece of fish and flapped it in Isadore's direction before feeding it to Prudence. "*He* should learn to be nicer to the Holder of the Haddock." Izzy flicked his tail.

"Yes, yes, here's yours."

After a while she blew out the lantern and crawled under the blankets to wait. Orange light came in through the cracks in the chimney stones. The garret was always smoky, but at least it was never completely dark. When at last she heard something it wasn't any of the familiar sounds that meant her aunt and uncle were preparing for bed.

Someone was knocking at the front door of the cottage.

Impossible. The sky had been dark for hours now. But there were her uncle's heavy footsteps crossing the room and the sound of the door being unbarred and quickly opened, then just as quickly shut and barred again. There was a subdued babble of voices, then more footsteps and the sound of benches being scraped back at the table. A man was speaking. Uncle Jock, or the visitor? She couldn't make out the words.

Once more, Annie eased open the trapdoor. The room below was red with firelight. A man sat at the table across from Uncle Jock. His back was to her, but she could see that he had narrow shoulders and a pointed head covered by wisps of straw-colored hair. Uncle Jock poured himself and the other man a cupful of whisky. Aunt Prim sat in the chair by the fire mending a pair of socks. She made a big show of measuring and snapping off thread, but Annie knew she was listening.

Uncle Jock was doing most of the talking. He finished his drink quickly and poured himself another. A musket leaned against the table by the strange man's side. From time to time he caressed it absently, as though it were a pet dog. Uncle Jock poured himself a third drink. He began to wave his hands around in big gestures, his eyebrows raising and lowering dramatically. She caught a few of his words: *strong, sorry, worth, quarry.* Suddenly Uncle Jock laughed and pounded his fist on the table.

"It's a deal, then!" he cried. The other man reached out and laid his hand over Uncle Jock's. It was a light touch, almost gentle, but a spasm of fear crossed Uncle Jock's face.

"Not like the first," the man said. "I want the living child."

Uncle Jock managed the barest of nods. Before releasing it, the man gave Uncle Jock's hand a couple of soft pats. *There, there.*

Uncle Jock snatched back his hand and rubbed it with the other hand as if to warm it.

The man rose to leave.

"Wait! You wanted to know about anything unusual, right? Any odd marks?"

"On the girl? Yes."

"Not on the girl, but . . ." Uncle Jock spoke in a rush. "Kinderstalk got into the neighbor's yard and left behind a tuft of white fur." He looked up hopefully. "That's unusual, isn't it?"

"Indeed. Any signs in your own yard?"

"My yard! No, none. None at all."

The man drew a purse from his pocket and shook out a handful of ringstones. Even from her perch, Annie could see that they were high quality, perfectly smooth and bright white. He took a single stone from the pile and poured the rest back into the bag. He placed the stone in front of Uncle Jock.

"To whet your appetite." He paused. "If anyone asks, kinderstalk took the girl."

The visitor paused on the threshold to light his lantern. Cold black air blew into the cottage. Then, quickly, he turned back toward the room, as if he had just remembered something. For the first time, Annie saw his face. She gasped, a tiny sound, but his head jerked toward her, and for a second their eyes seemed to meet. Then he smiled, the lipless mouth opening onto two rows of perfectly square white teeth.

"A good night to you," he said, and stepped out into the darkness.

Uncle Jock lunged at the door and slammed it shut.

Aunt Prim looked up from her mending. "When, Jock?"

"Tomorrow."

Aunt Prim nodded. "When she's finished her morning chores."

ॐ

Firelight colored the room a vivid orange. Deep shadows gathered in the corners where the light didn't reach.

Annie stood with one hand on the ladder. She could still climb back up, climb back into bed and curl up with the cats and wait for daylight to make sense of things. But daylight wouldn't bring sense, only the Drop. She thought of her old friend Gregor. Annie had been on her way to his house with a gift for his ninth birthday: a rock impressed with a bird's footprint; some kind of gull, she thought, though Gregor would know for certain. A wagon had passed her going the opposite way, and she remembered thinking it odd that they had put up the rain cover in clear weather. When she reached his house she found his mother standing alone in the yard, weeping. Later, over dinner, Aunt Prim told her, "I have bad news for you. The kinderstalk have eaten that friend of yours. Last night. They ate his shoes, everything. Now, no crying. It's a fact of life we must all accept."

"But I saw . . . ," Annie began, but Page caught her eye and shook her head.

Later, Annie lay with her head in Page's lap. "Did the kinderstalk really eat Gregor?"

"Monsters got him, I can tell you that much. But not you. I won't let them get you."

Annie still had the gull rock, pocketed in the hem of her dress. It kept the skirt from blowing around in strong winds.

She would need to be ready before her morning chores. And because she had never, in all her life, managed to wake up earlier than Aunt Prim, that meant she needed to be ready tonight. The only food she could find was a handful of dusty rinkle nuts that her aunt had been threatening to cook for a month. Now: money, rifle, and then the last, the most important, thing.

Of course the trunk was locked, but Annie hadn't lived twelve years in this house without learning a thing or two. Aunt Prim kept the key in *The Book of Household Virtues*, tucked between page 786, "Vinegar in the Use of Removing Blood Stains," and page 787, "Vinegar in the Use of Curing Barn-foot." When Page was alive, Aunt Prim used to make them sit after dinner and listen to recipes, medical cures, or worst of all, favorite sayings:

Hard work and no complaints turns chaff into wheat.

Quiet mouse gets the apple; noisy mouse chews the pip.

If a cow wanders into the yard, be quick to shut the gate.

Always, before she closed the book, Aunt Prim turned to the page in the back where she wrote down the names of children eaten by kinderstalk: Phoebe Tamburlaine was the first, followed by Cowley Crawford, Meg Winters, Walter Rout, and on and on until the last, Gregor Pepin. Annie couldn't resist looking at the page now. To her surprise, there were more than a dozen new names added after Gregor's. Beside each name Aunt Prim had printed the date of death and another number. Gregor's number was nine, the same as most of the children listed before him. But the numbers beside the children listed after him got smaller and smaller, and the dates of their disappearances closer and closer together. The last name was Minnie Wythe, taken a month past, age three.

❧

The trunk was nailed to the floor at the foot of her aunt and uncle's four-poster. Aunt Prim slept in the narrow slice of bed between Uncle Jock and the wall. Uncle Jock's huge feet, kicked free from the blankets, gave off a smell of wet wool. Annie knelt in front of the trunk and eased the lid open. Linen. But underneath the linen was hidden a smaller chest, tightly buckled with leather straps. She had seen it once before.

Aunt Prim had stepped out to the privy; Uncle Jock was off cutting.

"Annie, quick, I want to show you something." Page was kneeling over the trunk, her face flushed.

"What is it?"

"Proof."

The ringstone was beautiful, most of it a soft brilliant

pink, with some stones reflecting mauve and green tones. Colored stone was less valuable than white, but Annie thought it much nicer to look at.

"Proof of what?" Annie whispered.

"That Uncle Jock is as bad as we think. There's Aunt P. Hurry!"

❦

Annie opened the chest. *I'll only take what I need. Only a few, and only the darkest.* But there was nothing inside. Not one stone. She looked around the spare cottage in disbelief. Had he spent it all? There had been enough stone in that chest to buy a farm like Uncle Jock's twice over.

There was nothing else of value in the cottage. Nothing, unless—did she dare?

Every night before bed Uncle Jock dropped his clothes on the floor and put on his long underwear, and every night Aunt Prim picked up his clothes and put them away in the dresser.

After the man left, Uncle Jock had poured himself another drink and patted his knee.

"Come here, Prim, and have a look at this." He held the white ringstone up to the light. "I've never seen anything like it."

Aunt Prim put aside her sewing, but she sat on the bench, not his lap.

"It's so beautiful!" She smiled, and almost looked beautiful herself. "It's how I imagine a star might look. A fallen star."

She reached for the ringstone but Uncle Jock raised it over his head.

"Tut, tut, Primmy. This is my special burden."

Aunt Prim scowled. "Is it from the Drop?"

"Could be. Awfully fine for the Drop, though. Awfully fine."

"What did he mean about whetting your appetite, Jock? This was to be the end of it."

"We'll be free, my wild Primrose. We'll be free." Then he kissed not his wife but the stone, and tucked it into his front shirt pocket.

It would be easy enough for Annie to get his shirt from the dresser and the white ringstone from the pocket of his shirt, except for one thing. Uncle Jock had made the dresser, and Uncle Jock was as lazy about carpentry as everything else. The drawers squeaked.

He's had five cups of whisky at least. Five cups! That should keep him snoring. Still, Annie's heart beat faster as she eased open the first drawer. Socks and underpants. She tried the second. There it was, neatly folded but still smelling sourly of her uncle.

Aunt Prim was right. The white ringstone was as beautiful as a star, so clear and brilliant she almost expected it to give off heat.

The stone in her pocket made her feel bold and she shut the drawer too fast. The drawer jammed, the dresser shuddered, and *The Book of Household Virtues* toppled to its side with a bang.

Uncle Jock was on his feet in an instant. "Kinderstalk!" he roared, aiming his rifle at the dresser. When he saw Annie standing there he dropped the muzzle.

"You?"

Annie looked at her uncle and then at the book. Her mind said, *What if you miss?* But her hand knew what to do. The book struck him full in the face. He yowled and doubled over. Annie darted past him to the bed and thrust her hand between the mattress and the frame. Her eyes found Aunt Prim's stricken face, then she was across the room and up the ladder to the garret.

Annie half kicked, half dragged the heavy old mattress over the hatch, then stood on it for good measure. But what now? Already Uncle Jock was pounding on the door, lifting the mattress higher with each blow. One hand appeared through the hole. He heaved a shoulder through, then reached around and groped for Annie's ankle. She cried out and leapt clear of him, but soon his head and torso were visible. Annie looked desperately from her uncle to the window and back again.

"Don't you do it, girl!" Uncle Jock shouted. The nose of his rifle emerged through the trapdoor. She had no pistol, no knife, nothing.

Her uncle must have had the same thought, because he began to laugh. Blood trickled from a cut over his eye.

"You're caught now, kitten."

Annie snatched up her cloak and lantern, stuffed her feet into her boots, and threw open the window. Outside, though she couldn't see it, was the steeply slanting roof of the passageway that led to the privy. Prudence streaked out and Annie wriggled after her. Isadore stayed back. Annie's front end came through all right but her hips stuck in the window frame. Uncle Jock had one knee through the trapdoor now. Desperately, Annie pushed against the window frame with her free hand and kicked with her legs like a swimmer. Still she didn't budge. A hand closed around her ankle. She kicked frantically with the other foot and caught him in the throat. He gasped and coughed and then, with a shout of pain, let go of her leg. Her hips slid through. Before the darkness swallowed her she got a glimpse of orange fur flying and her uncle's fingers pressed to his cheek.

She was outside, after dark. She was *outside*. The roof's sharp peak pressed into her belly. For a long moment she just hung on, too terrified to move. Then a pair of familiar green eyes glinted ahead of her, reflecting the faint light from the garret window. Prudence.

Annie inched along in the direction of the cat. Now she could smell the privy, and feel the flat boards of the privy roof under her hands. Prudence disappeared and Annie stopped, groping forward with one hand. There was the edge of the roof, and the empty air beyond it. Starting at her waist, she walked her fingers carefully up her side until she found them: twenty-two pilfered matches, nestled in a pocket against her rib cage.

The lantern light penetrated no more than a few feet in

any direction, not enough to see the ground below—How far was it? Six feet? Ten?—but enough to see Izzy's orange forehead and white chin as he came up beside her. She felt the slight disturbance of air as he leapt from the roof. Then she held her breath and jumped after him into the darkness.

Chapter 2

Annie landed hard on her feet, then staggered forward onto her knees. The lantern sputtered but did not go out. Then she was up and running, the tip of Isadore's tail just visible ahead of her within the halo of lantern light. Prudence was waiting for them at the yard gate. Annie balked. *Leave the yard?* But the cats ran on.

"Prue, Izzy!" Annie ran and ran, stumbling over rocks and tree stumps, until she felt the sting of pine needles lashing her face.

"Izzy, wait!"

In front of her was the forest, behind her the cleared ground of her uncle's land. Annie took a step forward and stopped. Impossibly, the air here seemed denser, blacker than the air where she had just been standing. She could hear her own breathing, the *who-whooing* of an owl, the wind sifting the pines. Then, behind her, came a *thud, thud,* pause, *thud thud,* the sound of a big man running, stopping for a moment, then running on. A light bobbed in the distance, moving steadily closer.

Annie looked frantically toward the forest, then back at the approaching light, then toward the forest again. The forest belonged to the kinderstalk. Whatever the people of Dour County took by way of lumber, the kinderstalk took back: in livestock, in human life.

The thudding grew louder, until she could hear the crunch of stones under her uncle's boots. She looked down at the cats. They were sitting just within the ring of light from her lantern, staring up at her calmly. *Oh, not this. Anything but this.*

She opened the little glass door in the lantern and blew out the light.

The darkness roared over her, a landslide, an avalanche. The black air, heavy as earth, filled her throat and banked in her lungs. Her eyelids, too, felt heavy, as though caked with darkness. With effort, she closed her eyes and opened them, but there was no difference between the two.

Uncle Jock's footsteps paused a moment in confusion, then started up again more quickly than before. Annie dropped to her hands and knees and began to crawl through the dark. The cats pressed close. When her knuckles scraped bark, she grabbed the trunk and inched her way around until she felt she must be on the opposite side from where she had started. The light from Uncle Jock's lantern paused at the edge of the forest. She could see him now, or the parts of him the lantern illuminated, pacing back and forth: now his greasy hair, now his patched pants, now the glint of the long rifle he carried over his shoulder. Once she saw his face. He looked terrified.

So he fears that man more than this, more than the dark, more than the . . .

Uncle Jock turned suddenly and plunged toward her through the trees. Annie ducked behind the trunk and wrapped her arms around her knees, making herself as small as she could.

He raised the lantern and glared into the darkness.

"*Girl!*"

Uncle Jock put his rifle to his shoulder and fired. He jammed another bullet down the barrel and fired again. One heavy boot crunched down on Annie's hair. She clenched her teeth and kept silent. For long minutes, Uncle Jock went on firing shot after shot into the darkness, pausing only to reload and take new aim at whatever it was he hoped to kill.

Then, as if in answer to the shots, the kinderstalk began to howl. First one, a long, single note, then another and another, until they grew into a chorus. There was no telling how many there were, or how far away. Annie imagined one for every tree in the forest, thousands upon thousands, all moving toward this one place, all moving toward her.

Quiet, quiet, quiet, she thought, to keep her fear inside.

The lantern shook in Uncle Jock's hand, spilling light among the pines. Slowly he lowered his rifle. He took a step back. One voice separated itself from the rest, high and thin, very close by. *A female,* Annie thought, and wondered at the thought. What did it matter?

With a muffled cry, Uncle Jock spun on his heel and began to run back toward the cottage. The howling stopped, but now Annie heard a different sound. It began as a sort of hiss, then grew to a murmur, the sound of water over rocks. The first body brushed past her. A second followed, so close she could smell its mingled scent of blood and pine sap. Five passed, now six, without seeming to notice her. But kinderstalk could see in the dark. Surely they had spotted her? Smelled her? A seventh passed, then stopped. Shaking, biting her lip, Annie waited for the attack. Something blunt and soft touched her shoulder, and she heard not a snarl but a whine. Then silence. The thing was gone.

Annie's fingers trembled so badly she had to try three times before she was able to light the lantern. Part of her strained toward the cottage—had they reached him? Was Aunt Prim safe? But another, stronger part urged her away, while she still had a chance. The lantern shone on Prudence and Isadore sitting among the roots of the tree, looking at her as calmly as before.

"What now?" Annie whispered. Izzy turned and trotted deeper into the wood.

❧

They walked for what felt like miles, crossing streams, zigzagging through thickets. She tried to concentrate on where they were going, to remember her way back, but the dark made a fool of memory. She cowered at every scuffle in the undergrowth, every birdcall, but the kinderstalk did not show themselves again. *Because of Uncle Jock. They're still . . . don't think it!*

At last Isadore stopped at the base of an old oak tree. The trunk was so thick that five people holding hands could not have reached all the way around it. Hundreds of branches, some thicker than her entire body, some as slender as her smallest finger, stretched up into an infinity of black sky. Prudence sat between Annie's feet and together they watched Isadore scramble up the trunk like a squirrel. Annie looked down at Prue, who twitched her tail. She tried to smile but the flesh of her face felt cold and heavy.

With a jump she caught hold of the lowest branch, then planted her feet against the trunk and walked herself up until she could hook her knees around the branch and scoot on top of it. The next branch was easier to grab, and she climbed steadily upward through the dark. The lantern illuminated little more than her hands and the end of her braid, swinging in and out of the circle of light. Once she became so disoriented that she had to stop and spit to be sure which way was down.

Izzy was waiting for her on a branch that was perhaps six inches wide and what felt like a hundred feet above the earth.

Annie frowned at him. *You want me to sleep here?*

In answer, he leapt from the branch toward the trunk and disappeared. The lantern revealed an opening in the trunk, not much larger than the window to her garret room. The space inside was far too small for her to lie down, but at least she could sit upright without hitting her head. Years ago, fire had blackened the inside of the trunk and now the walls shone dark and shiny in the candlelight. Spiderwebs crisscrossed overhead and droplets of sap, as hard and bright as amber, decorated the walls. Yellow and brown leaves carpeted the floor. Was this where the cats lived before they came to her? The thought made her feel safe and a little sad. Prudence wriggled into the space between her bent knees and chest and started to purr.

Annie held up the lantern. Only a stub of candle remained. She would have to be quick.

The book's cover was made of faded black leather like the top part of someone's old boot. The title, printed in the center in gold letters, read, *The Trap of Vice*, by Chilton Smalle. Annie turned to the first page.

Beware, my fellow men, the trap of Vice! She with her talons will rend your sense, your sensibility, Nay! Your very sovereignty! Turn instead to Virtue, to gently guide you.

Well, that was boring stuff. Annie flipped through the book until she came to the page with her sister's writing in the margins. The book stayed open easily here, as if Page, or perhaps Aunt Prim, had spent hours studying it. Chilton Smalle's words had been scrubbed away and the paper bleached dry, and then someone had written new words on top. The new text was written longhand, the writing blocky and precise like a child trying to show he had mastered his letters.

Annie couldn't read a word of it. The letters were decorated with dots and waves and strange fillips. Some of them more closely resembled pictures. Was that a tree? A raven? Page's notes filled the margins, but except for a few words Annie recognized—*slip, graft*—the notes didn't make any more sense than the rest. Page's handwriting had always infuriated Annie: so tiny, so perfect, even the ink splotches somehow charming. Annie's own handwriting looked like something scratched in the sand with a stick. But now—now she could hardly bear ever having resented Page for anything. Carefully she returned the book to her hip pocket.

There had been something else pressed between the book's worn covers: a lock of Page's hair, pale blond, almost white, long enough to wrap twice around her wrist. This Annie tucked into a pocket hidden between two buttons, right over her heart. Then she closed her eyes, to pretend it was only the regular dark of sleep coming, and blew out the light.

❧

A bird's cry woke her during the night. Prue's striped face peeped up from her lap. Annie stroked a finger down the cat's nose. *Funny I can see your stripes,* she thought. *Funny dream.*

❧

Thock! Thock! Thock!

Aunt Prim liked to wake Annie in the mornings by pounding on the trapdoor with her broom handle.

Thock! Thock! Thock!

Annie put her hands over her ears and tried to roll over. Her nose scraped something rough. The pounding continued, only it didn't sound so much like pounding as relentless tapping. And the pounding wasn't coming from beneath her, but from somewhere near her right ear. Annie opened her eyes. She could see bright blue sky and a fringe of gold leaves. She was not in her bed, and there was no Aunt Prim. Annie scooted forward and stuck her head outside the hole to look around. A woodpecker hammered away at the side of the tree, the feathers on his crest a red blur. He made her feel happy somehow. Just in time she spotted Isadore, pressed nearly flat on a branch above the bird.

"Izzy, no!"

The woodpecker flapped away. Isadore landed neatly in front of her and began to wash his paws as if nothing had happened. Annie glared at him but the light feeling around her heart remained. Then she looked down. They *were* a hundred feet in the air, maybe more. Prudence, standing on a branch about halfway down the tree, was no more than a dark dot.

The climb down turned out to be much easier than the climb up. It was almost fun, like walking through a giant jigsaw puzzle: a foot fitting here, a hand there, a shoulder pressed against the trunk for balance, a knee wedged into the crook of two branches. Annie did not feel afraid again until the very end, when both her feet were planted firmly on the ground. For there, at the base of the tree, deep vertical gashes had been made in the bark. Annie reached to touch the pale wood of the exposed trunk. The highest marks were more than twelve feet off the ground.

Annie had never seen so many trees so close together, or so many different kinds. Some she recognized: tall pines, like men with sloped shoulders, strong-armed oaks, fancy-dress maples. Others she had never seen even in books, twisted trees with black trunks and long mossy beards, trees with gray bark and scarlet leaves, yellowish trees with wood so soft her finger left a dent.

She unfastened her cloak and pushed it back over her shoulders. Most of the morning's chill had faded, which meant she had about six hours of daylight left. Enough time to get to town, surely, if only she knew what direction to take.

"Izzy?"

But Isadore was busy tidying the fur between his toes.

"Prue?"

Prue eyed a nuthatch and pretended not to hear.

She walked a few yards in one direction, but when she turned around and could no longer see the oak tree she felt afraid and retraced her steps. She tried another direction, but the cats did not follow so she hurried back. Fear squeezed her ribs. Every minute she remained here was another minute lost to the darkness.

A hawk screamed overhead, no more than a black dash against the blue sky. Hawks loved to hunt the cutting fields at the forest edge, full as they were of little dazed creatures knocked from their nests. She would follow the hawk.

She ate whatever she could find. Most of the plants in the forest were unfamiliar to her, but the bracka bushes she recognized. They grew everywhere in Dour County, in thick hedgerows along the roadways and in straggly clumps along the cliffs that overlooked the river. In summer, Annie filled milk pails with their fat purple berries. These berries were the last of the season, too small and hard for the birds to pick off the branches, and so sour they made her jaws ache. *At least I'm not eating porridge, or*—she watched Prue bat an insect to the ground and pounce on it—*or that.*

The trees had started to shed their leaves and blue sky showed patchily through the branches. Just ahead a stream ran through a small clearing. Annie knelt to drink. A face stared back at her with wild eyes and a ragged halo of hair. Quickly, she broke the surface of the water.

Annie sat back on her heels and wiped her mouth.

"Prue, aren't you thirsty—"

Prudence was standing several yards away, her body strangely stiff. The cat arched her back, flattened her ears against her head, and hissed. Isadore had seen it too, whatever it was, and darted upstream to crouch behind a stand of reeds. Annie scrambled after him.

❧

Prudence had disappeared. In her place stood a kinderstalk.

It was twice the size of a sheepdog, but rangier, with long legs and a compact body. Rusty black fur grew shaggy around its neck and shoulders. The head was large in proportion to the body, with a narrow muzzle and close-set gold-colored eyes. Those eyes scanned the clearing, pausing—or had she imagined it?—at the stand of reeds before moving on.

The creature yipped twice. A second kinderstalk appeared, and then two more. Soon kinderstalk were appearing as if out of the air, and they all made their way to the same place. They sniffed the ground and snuffled and whined, but except for the first, not one turned toward her. She didn't dare move, scarcely dared breathe.

Then something truly strange happened. A man walked into the clearing, carrying a musket and a bulging burlap sack.

31

He had a round, pale face and round, pale eyes that protruded slightly. But his mouth—it was like something drawn by a young child, a red line reaching almost ear to ear. The flesh around the lips bulged, as though the man held something in his mouth he could not swallow. Annie's heart hammered against her ribs. This was the man who had come to her uncle's last night. This was the man the king had named—had touched with his own gloved hand—to run the western mines. This was Frank Gibbet.

Gibbet dropped the sack to the ground. The first kinderstalk, larger than the others, stalked over to him and rose up on its hind legs. Annie closed her eyes, afraid to see what must surely follow. Nothing happened. When she opened her eyes, the beast was still balanced uncannily on its hind legs. Gibbet remained where he was, his musket now resting casually against one leg, the barrel pointing into the earth. The kinderstalk began to make a garbled noise, something between a bark and a whine. As Annie watched wide-eyed, Gibbet made a similar noise back. The kinderstalk dropped down on all fours and Gibbet reached into his bag. He pulled out a dead rabbit and flung it toward the circle of kinderstalk. It hit the dirt and one of them lunged forward and then backed away, snarling, before turning to run into the woods with the rabbit dangling from its mouth.

Gibbet pulled rabbit after rabbit from his sack. The kinderstalk snapped them out of the air and, one by one, disappeared into the wood. Finally there was just Gibbet and the large kinderstalk left, and one dead rabbit.

"A token of my esteem," Gibbet said in his own language,

and tossed the rabbit on the ground. The creature lowered its head and with great delicacy took the rabbit between its teeth. Just as carefully it laid the rabbit at Gibbet's feet and walked slowly from the clearing.

Gibbet stared after the kinderstalk for a long time. Then he picked up his empty sack and his gun and went away in the same direction he had come.

Annie crept from her hiding place. She could not shake the chill that had gone through her when she saw Gibbet and the kinderstalk standing together. Watching Gibbet's face she had felt a spasm of fear, but not for herself. She had been afraid for the kinderstalk.

As she walked, Annie noticed signs that Gibbet had come this way before: a leaf pressed into the earth by the heel of a boot, new growth snapped off the ends of branches. The trail wound upward for a bit, then ended abruptly at the top of a steep drop. An oak tree clung to the hillside, half of its roots exposed where the soil had washed away. Gibbet's footprints overlapped at the base of the tree, carried on to the edge of the wash where they overlapped again, and finally headed down the hill to the open field below.

Annie had been so intent on trailing Gibbet it took her a moment to realize where she was. The cutting fields spread below her like a brown lake. Stumps of every size stuck out of the bare ground. At the northern end of the fields whole trees lay on their sides, leaves softening into mulch. To the west, where the road from Gorgetown abutted the field, stacks of chopped firewood sat waiting to be hauled away.

She had been here twice before, once with a pail of fish sandwiches her uncle had forgotten to take for lunch and another time exploring with Gregor. They hadn't wanted to come back.

No one cut alone. The men worked in pairs or groups, taking turns cutting and keeping guard. Uncle Jock had been her father's partner.

Page had told her the story a hundred times but Annie was never satisfied.

"Again?" Page would ask in mock exasperation. "Very well. Come here."

It was autumn, two years after their mother died. Their father and Uncle Jock had been cutting long hours all week. Uncle Jock wanted to cut extra wood and drive east to sell it. Father said no, no more than the family needs for winter. They were fighting when they left that morning. Aunt Prim hadn't expected them back until near dark, but Uncle Jock returned alone only a few hours later. He barred the door behind him and leaned his whole weight against it.

"Prim. Primmy. They took Shar."

"Took him! In broad daylight?"

"Only a moment I stepped away, only a moment. And there it was, and his clothes on the ground in tatters."

"Are you hurt, Jock? Should I fetch Grandmother Hoop?"

He held his big hands in front of his face. They were shaking. "It never touched me."

Annie wondered what it had been like to die here. Was he terrified? Was it painful? Gregor once told her the kinderstalk ate

34

you a piece at a time, starting with your feet. She thought of Uncle Jock. Had he reached the house in time?

And then, improbably, there he was, jogging across the field. Annie ducked behind the precarious oak. A second man appeared, walking swiftly from the opposite direction. Both men carried rifles. They reached each other and spoke briefly, heads bent. Uncle Jock pointed to the hill. The other man shrugged and they turned and walked toward her. They stopped near the base of the wash. Uncle Jock had been holding the other man's elbow, and now the man shook off his hand impatiently.

"You said you have a message for him?"

This was far and away the most hideous man Annie had ever seen. His skin was gray and thick and full of holes, like poured wax, with little round black eyes stuck into it. A puffy white scar parted his hair, as though someone had tried to split his head open with an ax.

"This." Uncle Jock produced a purse and pressed it into the man's hand. "We sold our cow for it this morning. It's all I've got."

The scarred man cocked his head to the side. "What happened to the child?"

"She's dead."

"Dead? This one too?"

"Look, how long do they last? A year? Two?" He jabbed a finger at the purse. "That should cover her take for the first few months. I can get more. I just need time."

The man tossed the purse lightly from hand to hand. "He won't like it."

Uncle Jock licked his lips. "I know he wanted her alive. I know. But he can be reasonable, yes? He understands about accidents. He understood before."

"I was there before," the scarred man said. Then his eyes narrowed. "What happened to your face?"

Uncle Jock raised his hand to the scratches on his cheek. The cut over his eye looked puffy and discolored.

"A branch, maybe, while I was cutting. It's nothing. So are we square, then? Am I square with him?"

"How did she die?" asked the scarred man.

"Kinderstalk. How else? We had a fight, she ran outside after dark. There's the end of it."

"Not quite."

"What do you mean?"

"Isn't there something you've forgotten?" The scarred man put out his hand. He wiggled his fingers.

Uncle Jock blanched. "It's gone."

"Where?" the scarred man asked sharply.

"The girl. The girl stole it."

"That stone was your pledge, Jock. You've gone and lost your pledge."

"I didn't ask for any pledge."

"He'll be sorry to hear that."

"No, don't tell him," Uncle Jock said quickly. He was wiping his hands over and over on his pant legs. "Are we square?"

The scarred man shrugged. He turned to go. "There is one thing, for next time."

"What? What is it?"

"You know he likes proof."

"Proof?"

"A finger might be anyone's. Better to take an eye."

Annie watched them leave, the scarred man brisk, Uncle Jock slouching off like a beaten dog. Izzy had come to stand beside her. He flicked his tail.

"I know," Annie whispered. "Part of me wished they'd caught him too."

Chapter 3

If I catch you in my store one more time, I'll feed you to the kinderstalk myself. Just see if I won't."

"And I'll help her. Truth's my witness."

Annie pushed back the heavy tangle of hair covering her face and sat up. Two figures loomed over her, one skinny, one stout.

"Oh! Well now, that's the last straw. That is the *very* last straw!" Annie followed the woman's gaze. One of the flour sacks she'd been using as a mattress had burst. Dozens of little white footprints covered the floor.

"Stealing my food, messing my place, and now vermin!"

"They're not verm—," Annie started to say, then gave up. She couldn't blame them. They'd been nice enough the first morning. Old Man Mutts had even given her a taste of spirits, "To bring you back to the living, gal." But it had been nearly a week now of sneaking between the tavern and Miss Gilly's shop, stealing food and sleeping in corners.

"I'll go," Annie said. Miss Gilly glared.

"I promise."

Standing on the edge of the village green in the cold morning air, Annie wished she could take the promise back. Aside
from the tavern and Miss Gilly's, the only shops not vacant
belonged to Beard, the blacksmith, and Mr. Crake, who carved
headstones. Across the green the church squatted sadly in the
middle of its crowded churchyard. The roof of the schoolhouse
was just visible behind the church, boarded up years ago for
lack of pupils. Perhaps she could hide there. *And then what,
Annie? Hide forever?*

"Ha! Little gal! Yes, you. Care for a chuff? It'll warm you."

Grandmother Hoop was sitting on a wooden bench smok-
ing her pipe. Between puffs she arranged her vials and jars on
the seat beside her. She didn't have a proper store, but Grandmother Hoop did even more business than Old Man Mutts.
She offered the pipe to Annie.

"No thank you, Grandmother."

"Suit yourself. But you could use some warming. Right
here." Grandmother Hoop rapped her knuckles against her
skinny chest. She studied the array of bottles for a moment,
then chose one and tapped a few grains of red powder onto the
heel of her hand. She pressed her hand up against a nostril and
sniffed hard.

Then she laughed, showing wet pink gums.

"Ha! That one's not for you. I've got something else for
what ails you."

She held up a vial filled with oily black liquid. "Now
this . . ."

Annie shook her head vigorously.

"Very well, very well. Another one dead this week past, did you hear? An older child, older than they usually take them. Dawdled on the way home, or so her auntie says. Wouldn't trust that sly weasel in *my* hen house, mind you . . ."

It took Annie a moment to register that *she* was the dead child in question, which made Aunt Prim the sly weasel. She liked Grandmother Hoop rather more now.

The old woman looked at her narrowly. "Who are your people, child?"

"I have no people." The words sounded awful, but Annie didn't feel awful saying them.

But Grandmother Hoop looked afraid. Her eyes darted around the green. "Run, child. Get away from here."

"But where? Where should I go?"

"Take the eastern road. Stay close to the ditch. If you see a wagon coming, you jump in that ditch and lie down till it passes. Otherwise don't stop until you cross the line into Broad County. Don't stop for anything, you understand me?"

"Yes, Grandmother." As Annie turned to leave, Grandmother Hoop caught her hand and pressed the vial into it. "Take this. Drink it. For the heart and for the belly."

❦

Annie had never been so far east before. The bare, rocky landscape of the coast gave way to gentle hills. Reddish grass poked through the dirt. Where the road wound closest to the wood she could hear the thud of the cutters' axes. On her uncle's map of Howland the forest covered Dour County like a storm cloud, the cross-hatched lines of ink blurring into solid black in the map's northwest corner. There the land bulged into the sea like a fist. Finisterre, it was called, the nest of the kinderstalk.

But moving east, as Annie was, the cloud of forest floated up to the top of the map, thinner and thinner. By the time you reached Magnifica no more than an inch of black ink showed along the northern border. By the time you reached the east coast, the forest had dwindled to nothing. Annie wondered what it would be like to follow this road all the way to the beaches of the eastern sea.

"Flat for miles and covered in sand," Page told her.

"Sand?" Annie had been skeptical. In Dour County, the cliffs dropped straight into the water.

Page grinned. "Pink sand. Pulverized ringstone."

"Ringstone sand?"

"Well, all kinds of stone." Page read aloud, "Granite, quartz, shiproke—but there's enough ringstone mixed in to make it look pink. Pink sand, Annie! Someday I'll take you to see it."

She passed a string of abandoned farms, then a yard where a woman stirred laundry in a tub of boiling water. Without thinking, Annie raised her hand in greeting, but the woman frowned and turned away.

She made a list of the things she had eaten in the past week. Bracka berries: many (sour). Rinkle nuts: one (inedible). Rum cakes: five (quite good). Rum drink: two sips (fiery). For the twentieth time, she took out Grandmother Hoop's vial and looked at it. *For the heart and for the belly.* She even opened it once—it smelled like fresh baked bread—but she was afraid to drink.

And then she saw it, just on the other side of the hill: whitewashed, gabled, with two full stories and a slate roof. But it wasn't the house that made her gasp and sway on her feet. It was the garden.

Yellow squash bumped sides with glossy orange pumpkins; blue eggplant gleamed among heads of pale lettuce. Between the house and barn grew rows of fruit trees bearing pink apples and flame-colored persimmons. Rose bushes, one red, one white, bloomed on either side of the cottage door. Around all of it spread a vast, perfect lawn, so that the house, the barn, the pumpkins all seemed to float in an emerald pool. A fence circled the lawn and contained it.

Without quite realizing how she had gotten there, Annie found herself standing outside the fence. The gate was unfastened. The cats had hung back, but now they rushed forward, whirring with agitation.

"Don't worry," she whispered. "Don't worry."

It only took a moment. As she left the yard, a swollen tomato in one hand, an apple in the other, Annie noticed for the first time that the top bars of the fence were smeared with tar. Shards of glass poked up from the tar like a set of jagged teeth.

An old chicken coop lay on its side where someone had

thrown it over the fence behind the barn. The door listed open and the wood had begun to break apart with rot. Decades of chicken droppings varnished the floor. It was the perfect place to eat lunch.

༄

Ox! Goose! Numbskull! Ditherer! And Page's favorite name for Uncle Jock, the vilest insult: *Soup-for-brains!* She should be across the county line by now. She should have kept walking and not stopped for anything like Grandmother Hoop told her. And what had she done instead? Taken a nap.

Annie groped for the lantern and matches. She kept her eyes shut tight, for she could tell by the feel of the air—heavy and soft against her lips and eyelids, like a cloth lain over her face—that night had fallen.

Her mouth tasted awful, her fingers and chin sticky with juice. At last she got the lantern lit. The candle was no more than a smudge of wax now, but she could see the cats well enough. They were sitting by the door of the coop, watching her.

Annie's heart sank. She tried anyway. "Come here, little Prue! Come here, Izzy!"

Izzy swatted her extended hand, claws not out but not entirely in. Stubbornly, she pulled him toward her and started to pet him.

"Ouch! Go on, then. Leave me here all alone. I hope the kinderstalk eat you. No I don't. Be careful."

She couldn't help staring after them, though it was pointless.

Or was that Prue stopping to look back, giving a little shake of her tail?

Of course it wasn't. Annie slumped down. The lantern's light could never reach so far.

～∾

They hadn't been gone long when she heard it, though time—like distance, like everything—was hard to measure in the dark. The first howl was answered shortly by a second, then a third and a fourth, until she lost count. How many? How close? She thought of the gashes in the trunk of the oak tree. The coop, which had been a small, lit world of its own, now felt like a trap.

The front door of the barn was locked, as she'd expected, but she remembered seeing a square opening just below the roof for pitching hay into wagons parked below. If only she had some kind of ladder, or . . . her toe struck something hard. Annie crouched down. A ladder. There were even notches cut into the ground beneath the window where the ladder's feet should go. But the ladder was big and heavy, and it took a long time and a great many scrapes, bangs, and thuds before she got it into place. *I might as well just howl to tell them where I am*, she thought, and started to climb.

A few steps up the ladder and the ground disappeared into blackness. Above her, too, was blackness. The same vertigo she had felt in the tree swept over her. Was she upright? If she fell, would she keep falling? The rungs under her hands and feet felt like the only things connecting her to the world she knew. Carefully, Annie stepped backward until she reached the ground and then started up again, counting.

"The ground is one rung down. Two rungs. Three rungs." She kept her eyes focused on her dirty knuckles, the wood grain of the barn wall.

"Nineteen rungs." She'd reached the top.

But the notches for the ladder had been in the wrong place. The pitching window was several feet to her right and a little above her, so she had to stretch to reach the window ledge.

She had one hand on the ledge and the other on the ladder when she heard him laugh.

"Like flies to honey," said the scarred man. "Every time."

He was carrying a torch and a rifle and smiling. "It's touching, really, how you all count the rungs. But you're gutsier than most, little"—he squinted up at her—"what are you now? A girl? You're gutsier than most, to try it in the real dark."

Then casually, almost lazily, he kicked the ladder. It tipped away from the wall and stood on its own for a moment, then fell backward with a *whoosh*. Annie let out a hiccup of pain as the weight of her body dragged against her arm.

"Now climb back down here at once, young lady!" The man scolded in a schoolmistress voice, then laughed. "Oh, if you insist. It's been weeks since I had any good target practice."

He fired before Annie could speak, or even think. The bullet whizzed past her hip and embedded itself in the side of the barn with a splintering sound. To her astonishment, she did not let go of the window frame.

"Oh, come now. I won't let you break your little bones." Another bullet hit the barn wall, a few inches above her head this time. Annie held on.

When he spoke again all the humor had left his voice.

"I can part your hair with one of these. Do you want a scar like mine?" Another bullet, so close to her face she could feel its trail of heat. "Do you?"

She let go.

He caught her. It was worse than hitting the ground. His arms were harder than wood, and he smelled bad—not of sweat and manure, as she'd expected, but of a ripe, almost rotten sweetness. Annie started to struggle and kick. He dropped her, no, he tossed her, to the ground. By the time she had scrambled upright he had the nose of the rifle pressed into her spine.

"This way."

His torch cast enough light that she could walk without stumbling, but Annie dragged her feet. This would be her one chance to get away, before they got to wherever they were going. If she could just find something to distract him . . . oh, where were the cats?

"I wouldn't waste the thought, gal. There's nothing but forest to the north of us, and miles to town. But don't worry, you'll be snug as a bug where you're headed, snug as—" He stopped. "What is . . . ?"

The kinderstalk had started to howl again, but the sound

had a different quality from what Annie had heard in the chicken coop. Those howls had sounded like questions, she realized now, questions and answers. These were fierce, urgent. And closing in.

"Move!" The scarred man grabbed her arm and started to run, half carrying her across the yard. He stopped at a wooden door in the ground with a ring in the center.

"Lift it up."

He watched her struggle for a few seconds, then reached down and pulled the door free with one hand. A ragged circle opened in the earth.

"In."

"No."

He looked at her in real surprise. "You don't hear them? You think you're better off out here?"

"I won't. You'll have to shoot me first."

Behind them, a kinderstalk snarled. The man whirled around, firing his rifle wildly into the dark. Then, quick as a snake, he turned and struck Annie behind the knees with the barrel.

"No good to us dead," he hissed.

She pitched forward, the black mouth of the pit opening wide to swallow her.

Chapter 4

A beetle inched past Annie's nose. Dirtcarver, or maybe a mudmopper. Gregor would have known. She poked the beetle and it melted into the darkness. Her head hurt, and her shoulder, and her hip. She eased herself into a sitting position and did a quick inventory of limbs. Nothing broken, but she'd taken quite a knock. Her eyesight kept shifting between clear and blurry, and the light had a queer brown tone to it. She held her hand in front of her face: five fingers, just as usual. She straightened her arm and the hand disappeared into the dark. Bent her elbow, the hand came back. She supposed she should blow out the lantern. It was a wonder the candle had lasted as long as this.

The lantern lay on its side a few feet away. Reluctantly, she reached for it.

Annie snatched back her hand as if stung.

The handle of the lantern was cool. The glass windows of the lantern were dull and cold. The candle had burned to nothing. And yet she could see the bit of string that tied the end of her braid, and the matted hair above it. She could see the coarse gray fabric of her dress spread out across her lap, down to the pucker in the cloth where Page had darned it. She could see the dotted lines of dried blood on the backs of her hands where bracka bushes had scratched her. Annie squeezed her eyes shut and the world went dark. She opened them and there were her hands still in her lap, gripping the fabric of her dress tightly now. She picked up the lantern and examined every inch of it, but there was no denying that it was not lit and had not been for some time.

The light must be coming from overhead, or behind her, or . . . Annie scrambled around the confines of the pit, objects coming into view as she got nearer to them, sinking back into darkness as she moved away.

The dirt walls formed a rough circle that narrowed toward the top, with the underside of the wooden door forming the roof. The floor was about as wide across as she was tall. To one side was a bucket, to the other a filthy blanket full of holes and a heap of moldy vegetable rinds. Neither the door, nor the walls, nor the blanket, nor the bucket emitted any light. Desperately, Annie kicked the vegetable rinds, but they were just vegetable rinds.

She studied her hands again, holding her right wrist with her left hand to keep it from shaking. If she kept her hand close to her face, she could see every detail: the sworl of prints on each fingertip, the branching lines on the palm that Grandmother Hoop claimed she could read to foretell a person's future. When she moved her hand away, its outlines grew softer, the surrounding light deeper and deeper brown, as though she were submerging her hand in murky water. Each time she repeated the experiment she thought she could see her hand a little longer before it disappeared. Something like fascination crept into Annie's chest alongside the fear, but she squashed it.

I hit my head. This won't last. It's . . . it's . . . She struggled for the words Page would use, words from her books that made things sound exotic but comfortingly remote, easy to shut up and put away, like the books themselves. *It's a conundrum. It's an oddity. It's an aberration.*

If a cow wanders into the yard, be quick to shut the gate.

Not Page, but Aunt Prim, reading aloud from *The Book of Household Virtues*. For the first time in Annie's life the saying meant something.

A second inspection of the pit convinced her that the only way out was through the opening at the top. Standing, her head just grazed the wooden door. She pressed her palms flat against it and shoved as hard as she could. It didn't budge. So this was why the scarred man had wasted those precious seconds watching her struggle with the door, to be sure it was too heavy for her. She yelped in a sudden rush of anger and panic and pushed again with all her strength. Then she felt it, a slight vibration against her palms, the *strick, strick* of nails against wood.

Annie shrank back. The kinderstalk. Even here, they could smell her.

More scratching, then silence, and then a different sound, almost too faint to hear.

A meow.

"Izzy! Prue!"

The cats meowed again.

Annie sagged against the wall, then let herself slide down it until she was half sitting, half lying on the floor. All that long night, whenever she called out, they answered.

❧

The ax, or whatever the weapon had been, had split his head into two globes. A dense ridge of scar tissue ran between them, bumpy and faintly blue like thick ice. At first she had tried not to look—he couldn't help it, after all—but after a while she realized he *liked* the scar, the suggestion of violence it carried. When he spoke he dipped his head toward her, as if to ask, what do you suppose happened to the man holding the ax?

She'd had plenty of time to study him since he hauled her from the pit at daybreak and marched her back to the barn. He pushed her into a wagon and bound her ankles together, then looped a stout rope several times around her waist and tied the ends to one of a dozen metal rings fastened to the inside of the wagon bed. He fit the rain cover over the top and sides of the wagon.

Her hands he left free. Breakfast consisted of a wedge of bread, a blackened fish head, and a couple of knobby potatoes with bits of earth still clinging to them. Annie ate it all. And she drank from the bucket of water he'd given her, drank until her stomach swelled like a gourd. The water tasted of tin and damp wood and something else, something faintly sweet. She tipped the bucket nearly vertical to drain it.

"Oy!" The scarred man knocked the bucket away. "Easy now."

⁓

Annie was glad he'd tied her facing away from him because she was crying. She'd tried. She'd really tried very hard to avoid this, and it had come to nothing. Annie covered her face. Tears slid down her wrists into the sleeves of her dress. Worse than being bound like an animal, worse than what waited for her, was the fact of her own stupidity. She should have listened to Grandmother Hoop.

"You cry, if it makes you feel better," the scarred man said cheerfully. "After today, you won't have the energy to spare."

⁓

They drove west past Gorgetown, covering the very ground she had covered the day before. When they reached the cliffs they turned south, and the landmarks Annie recognized from her games with Gregor—the black rock jutting over the gorge like a giant anvil, the cluster of stones ringed with tonsure moss where they had buried the body of a bird—gave way to a flat, unchanging landscape of yellow dirt and scrub brush.

The first sound she heard was familiar, though out of place: the *thud, swing, thud* of ax against wood. There was a high, whirring noise she couldn't place, and a soft *tink, tink* that sounded like breaking ice. Then men's voices, and the unmistakable *gong!* of a dropped iron pot. The wagon rolled past a cluster of tents, then past a cooking area cluttered with dirty pots and pans and water buckets, then on past a group of men repairing baskets made from birch bark. The last thing they passed was a long, low building without windows, set somewhat apart from the rest of the camp. Thick smoke hung over the building, though Annie could see no chimney.

The wagon shifted as the scarred man got down from his seat. And then he was facing her, smiling.

"Welcome to the Drop."

❧

A bald man with a furry mole on his scalp hurried over.

"Chopper. He's here. Just a friendly visit, he says. Just a friendly visit."

Annie glanced at the scarred man. Chopper was his name? Well, it fit. He was looking past her, his expression anxious, almost wistful. She followed his gaze. Walking back and forth along the cliff top, his hands clasped behind him and his head tipped forward as though he were composing a poem, was Frank Gibbet.

The man with the mole glanced at Annie. "New catch? That's the third this month."

Chopper shrugged. "Hard times. Ask him if he wants to have a look at this one, since he's here."

While Chopper untied her, Annie kept her eyes on Gibbet. The man with the mole was a big fellow, taller than Gibbet, but the impression she had watching them was of Gibbet looking down at the other man, like a parent barely tolerating the ignorant questions of a child.

53

The men walked toward them. Annie wanted to hide, but Chopper stood behind her with his hands on her shoulders. Would Gibbet know her somehow? Would they find the white ringstone hidden in the hem of her skirt along with Gregor's rock? Or the vial from Grandmother Hoop, buried in a pocket within a pocket so deep it almost reached her knees? What about the lock of Page's hair, pressed over her heart?

Gibbet looked her over carefully. Annie looked anywhere but his face. He peered at the top of her head. He inspected the end of her braid. He lifted each of her hands and examined the fingernails. His hands were as rough and cold as granite.

"Turn," he said to Chopper, and Chopper turned her.

"Search," Gibbet said next, and Chopper led her to a sagging canvas tent. A girl with stringy hair and a face like a dinner plate waited inside. She helped Annie undress and handed her clothes out to Chopper, then walked around her in a slow circle while Annie shivered.

"Any marks?" Chopper asked when they'd finished. The girl shook her head.

Chopper held up Page's book. "*The Trap of Vice*, by Chilton Smalle. Serious little thing, isn't she?"

Gibbet frowned. "Anything else?"

Annie held her breath, but the only things Chopper had uncovered were the inedible rinkle nuts and a red leaf she had picked up in the forest. He crumbled the leaf in his fingers.

"That's all, sir."

"And no marks." Gibbet sounded disappointed.

"Put her in with the rest?" Chopper asked.

Gibbet shrugged and moved off, no longer interested. Chopper started after him. He was still holding Page's book.

"Wait, Mr. Chopper! Please, may I have my book?"

Chopper handed it to her with a faint smile. "Expect to get some reading in, do you? Think again, kiddie."

The two men spoke for some time, or rather Chopper talked and Gibbet listened, his red line of a mouth tightly closed. At length Chopper gave a brief salute and Gibbet walked to a waiting wagon. He had already taken the reins in hand, and Annie was thinking how odd it was that a person of his stature should drive himself, when a young man ran up and spoke to him. Gibbet bent toward him, as though listening attentively. Then casually, without anger, Gibbet raised his whip and slashed it across the man's face. He drove off, leaving the man rocking on his knees in the dirt.

The man with the mole said only, "Shouldn't have done it," then untied her and brought her over to stand at the very edge of the cliff.

"Now watch."

Iron rings had been driven into the rock at even intervals along the top of the cliff. From these rings stretched taut ropes, disappearing over the edge into the bare blue air. Men hung from the ropes at various heights along the cliff face, chipping at the rock with delicate picks. Around their hips they wore wide leather straps fashioned into a sort of seat, to which were attached woven baskets. They filled the baskets with the shards of ringstone they carved from the cliffs. From above the men looked like spiders dangling from silk threads, blowing back and forth across the surface of the rock with each strong breeze. While Annie watched, one man shouted a warning that he had dropped his pick. The pick grew tinier and tinier until it became invisible in the blue air above the blue river sweeping through the base of the gorge. She looked at the ropes straining against the weight of the men and their heavy baskets. Many of them had begun to fray where they rubbed against the stony cliff edge. One of the men hallooed from the end of his rope.

"Number Four, up!"

A man crouching at one end of the line of ropes repeated the cry. "Number Four, up!"

Three stout men appeared from inside one of the tents. Despite the cold morning air, they wore only brief tunics over their pants and no shoes. The muscles in their bare arms looked ready to burst through the skin. One of them wiped his mouth with the back of his hand, as if he had been drinking.

The men walked to where the ropes were tied off and sat down to put on their shoes. These were no ordinary shoes. Attached to the soles were metal spikes, three or four inches long and viciously sharp. The men stood in line, one behind the other, and began pounding their feet into the hard dirt. Then each man put his arms around the waist of the man in front of him, and the first man leaned forward to grasp the rope.

"Ready?" he called out.

"Heave!" The men threw their weight back simultaneously, and the rope inched up the cliff. The first man passed the slack in the rope back to the last man, who curled the rope around his arm.

"Ho!" the first man called, and the three men leaned forward together.

"Heave!" he called, and they all leaned back again.

In this manner, faster than Annie would have thought possible, they hauled man and basket up the cliff. Chopper squatted at the edge to watch the man's progress, his face impassive. Even before the man's head had come into view Chopper had retrieved his basket and carried it over to a set of scales. Amidst all the crude equipment of the camp, the sagging tents and dented pots, the scales looked as if they had come straight from the palace coffers: gleaming brass and calibrated to a fraction of an ounce.

Chopper was staring at the scales intently. He frowned and weighed the man's take a second and then a third time. The heap of stone gleamed with a soft, bright light that looked as if it came not from the reflected rays of the sun but from within the heart of the stone itself. And the color! Each tiny chip of stone burned with the full spectrum of colors, as though a rainbow had frozen and shattered into millions of pieces.

"Number Four, pat down."

At the sound of Chopper's voice Annie felt the man holding her jerk to attention.

The miner they had just pulled up was standing on his feet now. He was no more than skin draped over a skeleton; his hands, red and puffy from countless scrapes against the rock, looked too big for his body. While Annie watched, they removed each article of his clothing and inspected it. They looked in pockets and cuffs; they turned his long underwear inside out, poked into his socks. He had not been wearing shoes.

Annie found she could not look away from his feet. Like his hands, they seemed to belong to a different, much larger body. The frost that had covered the ground in the night had not yet burned away, and she thought how painful it must be, the ice touching his skin.

"Twenty minutes rest, Number Four, then start up at Thirteen," one of the men with spiked boots said. The naked man bent down to gather his clothes from the ground where the inspectors had dropped them. He turned and walked wearily toward the tents. Red welts covered his back, some of the cuts just beginning to scab over, others still oozing blood. Beneath these were the fainter marks of earlier beatings, and beneath those the thin white lines of long-healed scars.

The man with the mole took in Annie's expression with satisfaction.

"Light fingers, that one. A few days back we caught him with a chip under his tongue. Worth nearly a month's rent in Dour County. But you know that."

All the water she'd drunk on the way over began to roil in her stomach like the sea during a storm. Annie swallowed hard, but she could not swallow the awful sweetness filling her mouth. Chopper had come to stand in front of her. He placed his hands on her shoulders and looked down at her almost affectionately.

"Now you—you would never survive a beating like that. My men don't know their own strength. They can't tell the difference between a grown man and a child, once they get started."

Annie tried to twitch away, but Chopper held fast. "Do we understand each other?"

She looked him full in the face, then bent forward and vomited an ocean onto his feet. For several moments she remained bent over, staring at the partially digested fish head resting on the top of one of his boots. He didn't move, didn't react in any way, except by tightening his grip on her shoulders until she winced.

"Is the child diseased?" someone asked.

Chopper let her go. "Start her at Number Four. Smirch, my boots."

The man with the mole looked daggers at Annie but squatted down to do as he was told.

Hauler, though bigger and stronger than Chopper, was friendlier and stupider. He held her arm loosely. "Ready?"

"What is it you want me to do, exactly?" Annie asked, rather impressed by the coolness of her voice. Hauler stared at her blankly for a moment, then threw back his head and laughed.

"Hoo!" He wiped his eyes. "Fresh!" He patted her shoulder

with a huge hand. "I don't mind fresh, but daylight's wasting. Let's get you over that cliff and start cutting."

"I will not—," Annie began, but Smirch, red-faced, cut her off.

"This is a kindness, believe me, letting you learn in the day. Chopper must like you."

"Fresh," Hauler said again, as though that explained something. "And tall. Maybe head of the line?"

"Maybe." Smirch had picked up Number Four's rope and begun to tie a series of complicated knots at one end, fashioning it into a seat.

"Okay, step your feet in, like this." Hauler looked at her expectantly. Annie shook her head. He frowned, puzzled. "You want to go over without a harness?"

Annie gave in. Hauler showed her how to attach the leather belt to the rope seat, and then how to attach the basket to the belt.

"Boots off."

Annie kicked at his hand. He scowled. "Too fresh."

"Why are you taking my boots?"

"You'll see."

Then he picked her up by the harness and carried her, one-handed, over to the cliff edge.

"Now sit down with your legs straight out in front of you, and walk yourself backward down the rock."

Sit down into what? Annie thought. She looked over the edge into space. Far below she could see the blue river winding its way through the bottom of the gorge.

"If you don't climb down, I'll have to push you," Hauler said, making a sad face. Annie looked down again. The rope would run out of slack eventually, but how far would she fall before it did? Twenty feet? Fifty? She took a few small steps backward, until her heels stuck out over the edge of the cliff. Then slowly, slowly, clutching the rope with both hands, she began to sit back. She closed her eyes and imagined her uncle's chair with its enormous cowhide cushion waiting to catch her. When she was sitting flat, the bare air as a seat, she began to inch her feet over the edge and down the rock face. The slack in the rope ran through her hands as the rope grew longer and the faces peering at her over the cliff grew smaller.

" 'Atta girl!" Hauler yelled.

Finally, the rope ran out of slack. Annie hung there, fifty feet from the top, hundreds of feet from the bottom, literally in the middle of nowhere.

The air felt much colder here than at the top. Wind blew up from the bottom of the gorge, buffeting the men on the ends of their ropes. The pale sun of autumn, while scarcely bright enough to warm her, dazzled the rock face so that Annie had to squint to look at it. Most of the men wore hats pieced together from scraps of cloth and birch bark.

Men hung to the left and right of her, some closer to the top of the cliff, some more than a hundred feet down. The men did not talk or even look at one another. Annie felt in her basket for the chisel. It was sharply pointed at one end and blunt at the other, like a hammer. The routine seemed to be to whack the rock with the hammer end, then turn the tool around and chisel out the ringstone with the pointed end. Strike, spin, chisel. But where to strike first? She watched as one of the men closest to her began to push himself from side to side, gaining speed. He ran horizontally, backward and forward along the rock, until he gained enough momentum to leap over a bulge in the cliff face. He clung with expert fingers and toes to the rock on the other side of the bulge. By working his feet into cracks in the rocks he left his hands free to chisel at the vein he had spotted. So this was why they didn't wear boots.

Annie shivered. The wind never abated, cutting through her skirt, her petticoat, her woolen underwear, her socks. A pink gleam caught her eye. She clutched at the rock, finding fissures in which to anchor her feet. Sure enough, inches from her face was a fat vein of ringstone. Annie tapped at it gingerly with her pick. Nothing happened, so she whacked it. A chip of stone flew off. Annie tried to grab it with her free hand, but it slipped through her fingers and she tipped headfirst to one side. She gave a little scream and righted herself, clinging to the rock. When her heart had slowed down, she cautiously tapped at the ringstone again, experimenting until she could flake the stone off easily.

The basket at her waist grew heavier. Her fingers ached from gripping the pick. One by one the men on either side of her called to be brought up. When Annie finally looked up, rolling her neck to ease the ache, she saw that only one man was left on the cliff face with her. He worked about twenty feet above her, hanging lopsided from the weight of his basket.

"Number Five, up!" he called, his voice cracking with weariness. Chopper stuck his head over the top of the cliff.

"Keep working, Number Five. You were below quota last shift."

"Sir, respectfully, sir, I'm awful heavy. My rope looks bad, sir."

Chopper didn't answer. His head disappeared from sight.

The cliff was silent for several long minutes, except for the sound of the man's pick. Annie's basket was full, and she was about to call for someone to take her up when she heard the man above her cry out. His basket, groaning with stone, had pulled him nearly perpendicular to the rock face. As Annie watched in horror, the fibers of his rope began to stretch and snap, one by one.

"Five, up! Five, up!" the man shrieked, but it was too late. The last fiber of rope, frail as a human hair, snapped. The man hung suspended in the still air for one long, impossible moment, his mouth opening and closing, opening and closing. Then he fell, the basket bearing him down like a drowning man to the bottom of the ocean. He screamed as he fell, a long, high wail. Instead of fading away, the scream rose, spiraling up the gorge. Annie pressed her hands against her ears. She felt a sharp tug at her waist as they reeled her up. The scream went on and on.

⤞

Cold. Cold, cold, cold, cold, cold. But at last the screaming had stopped.

"Don't take it so hard, now. These things happen from time to time." Hauler set down the bucket. "We have a fellow who collects the fallen stone from the gorge," he added, as if that would help. He took a rag from his pants pocket and moved to pat her sopping hair.

"Get away from me."

"Now, now. You want a friend in me. You really do. I'm all the children's favorite."

Annie met his eyes. "Where?"

Hauler jerked his thumb toward the long, windowless building she had seen when she first arrived at camp.

"Why?"

"Why? Four solid walls! Real beds! It's a nice place, the orphanage. Nice and warm. You see what the men make do with?" His thumb shifted to indicate the rows of limp canvas tents. "Stacked like cordwood in there, when the real weather comes."

"I meant why haven't I seen any children? Where do they work?"

"They work right here, of course." Hauler handed her a blanket. He tipped his head to the side, regarding her. Then he smiled slowly, and Annie realized she had made a bad mistake, thinking him stupid.

"The children work at night," Hauler said.

⁓

At first the beds appeared to be empty, blankets flung across them or heaped at the head. Then one of the blankets stirred

64

and revealed a small hand, and Annie realized the beds were full of sleeping children.

Before he left her, Hauler had told her she could sleep through the first night shift.

"You had a nice take for a first timer. Chopper will be pleased." He pointed through the open door. "You can sleep there, middle bunk. Tell everyone to shove back one. We're a bit tight, but the babies can share." Then he had patted her shoulder and pushed her through the door. "Night-night."

❦

The construction of the orphanage could not have been simpler: two long walls, two short walls, a low-pitched roof. A door in the west wall that opened onto the path to the cliff. A door in the east wall that opened onto the privy. Three tiers of beds lined up along the south wall. No windows. No hearth. No lanterns. No light.

If a cow wanders into the yard, be quick to shut the gate.

She stood there stupidly until a bell clanged outside the door, startling her. The children all rose at once, as though they had not been sleeping at all, but waiting. The tallest child, a girl, slept closest to the door. She reached for a coiled rope hanging by her bed. Even in the dark, she moved with the confidence of long routine, but Annie could see her hands trembling as she uncoiled the rope. She tied one end to her wrist and passed the rope to the child behind her, who looped the rope around his wrist and passed it on, until the rope reached the smallest child. The boy, no more than three or four, struggled to make a knot, and Annie, unthinking, stepped forward to help him.

"Who is it? Who's there?"

"Is it the Chopper?"

"What's happening?"

The children buzzed with fear, knocking against each other in the dark. Annie kept still.

"Step out!" called out the tallest. "Step, step, step!"

At once they fell silent and marched behind her to the door. The girl rapped on it three times and it swung open. Torchlight flared through the opening and Annie felt rather than heard the faint *whoosh* of the children's collective relief. They marched out the door and the man holding the torch shut the door behind them.

Annie walked over to the bunk Hauler had told her to take. The blanket was still warm. She walked on to the very last row of beds, where the youngest children slept. She hadn't seen anyone climb down from the top bunk. Maybe she could sleep there.

But the bed wasn't empty. A boy lay still, his face very white. He kept his lips pinched together as though trying not to cry out. Annie wanted to say something to make him less afraid, but what could she say? *Don't worry, I can see in the dark?* His eyes rolled this way and that, trying and trying to see. The white hands clutching the edge of the blanket looked like the hands of someone very old. A thick scar covered one knuckle. The index finger of the left hand. Annie felt something flicker in her chest. He'd been holding the stick in that hand, whittling with the right when the knife slipped. Her own hand shaking, Annie touched the scar. The boy gasped.

"Gregor?"

Chapter 5

Gregor's skin had always been lighter than Annie's, but now the contrast was like snow against wood. Lying side by side on the bed, his feet came only to her calves. She might have circled his ankle with her hand.

"Gregor, have you been sick a long time?"

He hesitated. "When I heard you before, before I knew it was you, I thought they'd sent Smirch to get me. He's the one tosses you over when you run out."

"Run out?"

"Run out, wear down. Most of us don't leave here. You might go live in the tents when you get old enough, the boys, anyway. Or work the kiln. The girls go somewhere different, laundry or making blankets. I don't know." He took a shallow breath. "But most just run out. And then . . . someone will be sick, and in bed a few days. If they don't get better, one day you come off shift and they're gone and you don't know what happened. Meg—the tallest—Meg says Smirch throws you over." He frowned. "But I think they told her to say that."

"Why do they have children work? There are so many men."

"To fit the gaps."

"I don't understand."

He turned his head toward her. His breath smelled sour-sweet.

"Do you know why white stone is worth so much more than the rest? It's so deep in the rock. The sun and rain are what color the stone. It takes the men days to cut into where the white stone is. But there are gaps in the rock." Gregor held his hands up, the palms close together. "We can fit sideways."

She thought of the man they'd strip-searched, with his big hands and feet. Gregor's hands were big for his body, too. Her throat hurt.

"Do they try to keep you small?"

Gregor didn't say anything for a minute. "Even the gaps are chipping out now. Mostly just the really narrow ones left." He moved his hands so the palms nearly touched. "That's what the babies are here for."

"How do you—," Annie began, but Gregor shook his head. "My turn."

Annie's heart gave a hard thump. "You want to know—"

"—how you can see in the dark."

It felt so strange to hear him say the words. But comforting, too, as though this was just another thing in nature to puzzle over. How does a mole see underground? How does a dregfish see in the mud of the river bottom? How does a hawk see a mouse from a hundred feet in the air?

"I don't know," Annie said. "It just happened. I think it's getting stronger. I think I can see more and more." It was true. From where she lay, she could see a letter scratched in the wood of the opposite wall: "M." She squinted. The rest of the letters were there too, growing fainter as the carver ran out of energy: "-o-t-h-e-r."

"When did it start?"

She told him about the garden and the chicken coop and Chopper's trick ladder. He nodded, familiar with the story. "You spent the night in the pit?"

"That's when it first happened. Well, that's when I first noticed," she amended.

"You're lucky it was then."

Annie hadn't really thought about what it would have been like to be underground and unable to see.

"Like being buried alive," Gregor said.

"But not you."

"No. About half are runaways or lost. They catch some with the garden. It's the only road out of Dour County, you know. The rest are sold. Like me."

"At least you weren't so stupid as I was."

Gregor laughed. Annie liked the sound of it.

"Everyone says the pit is the worst of all. Worse than this." He flapped his hand to indicate the room, the dark.

Annie was thinking of the names from Aunt Prim's list.

"You said Meg is here—Meg Winters? And Cowley? They're all here?"

"Cowley's dead. But yes, Meg, and Walter, and all the rest,

and ones after me." He gave a funny smile. "Everyone the kinderstalk ate."

"Even Phoebe Tamburlaine? She must be old by now."

He shook his head. "No one's ever seen her, even the ones who've been here the longest. Maybe they really did eat her."

❧

Aunt Prim had never shown much interest in the children on her list, except for Phoebe Tamburlaine, the first.

"You know she only talks about Phoebe to scare you, right? To make you behave?" Page said to her one day.

"You mean it never happened?"

"I don't know. Something happened, but the version you heard probably isn't true. People like to exaggerate. Especially people like Aunt P."

"Oh." Annie had felt strangely disappointed.

Page smiled, and patted the mattress next to her. "Do you want me to tell you the version I know?"

Phoebe Tamburlaine lived with her parents and six siblings on a farm close to town. One day when she was behaving very badly, her mother shut her outdoors to learn a lesson. The sky was bright. The sun was hot. Phoebe's shadow moved around her body as the sun moved in the sky. "Mama?" Phoebe called, but her mother didn't listen, or didn't hear. Night fell. "Mama!" Her screams, if she had time to scream at all, were drowned by the frenzied howls of the kinderstalk. When her mother ventured outside the next morning she saw the dirt in the yard all pocked with paw prints; of her daughter there was nothing left but a tattered shoe and a single sock, flecked with blood.

"Beware the kinderstalk, Annie! Bewaaare!" Then Page had pounced on her and tickled her until she shrieked.

❦

Annie sat up. "Gregor, we can leave this place. They don't know I can see, and I have some terrible-looking stuff from Grandmother Hoop. We could give it to a guard, or—"

"Grandmother Hoop? What did she say it was for?"

"She said, 'for the heart and for the belly.'"

"Don't waste it. She cured my dad once. He was sick, awful sick. It was green powder and she mixed it with whisky. 'Tastes like frogs!' he said. But he got better, Annie. He got better quick."

"We won't use it on the guards then. But we have to plan. Tomorrow night I'll have to work, and if Smirch really . . ."

"Rest first, just a bit. Then plan."

With his eyes closed, she could see the prominence of the brow bones, the veins at his temple like distant rivers.

"Yes. Rest," she said. "I'm exhausted."

❦

Annie was just wondering if Gregor had fallen asleep when he spoke again, so softly she had to strain to hear.

"Darling, what do you wish for?"

"What? Gregor, are you . . ."

"Darling, what do you wish for? The dark is drawing near."

"Gregor!"

He nudged an elbow into her ribs, barely a touch.

She laughed. "Start again from the beginning. I'll be the child."

"Darling, what do you wish for? The dark is drawing near."

"A ribbon, Mother, a ribbon, to tie back my hair."

"Darling, what do you wish for? The dark is drawing near."

"A key, Mother, a key, to lock up my heart."

"Darling, what do you wish for? The dark is drawing near."

"A light, Mother, a light, to find you when you're far."

"Darling, what do you wish for? Tell me what you fear."

"The dark, Mother, the dark, the dark wood is what I fear."

When she knew he was asleep, Annie slipped from the bunk, careful first to cover him with both blankets.

No one had bothered to lock the door. And why would they? The children had no torches or lanterns of their own. They had no weapons. The dark imprisoned the children more securely than the highest, thickest wall. Annie shuddered, partly with the excitement of how easy it would be to escape, and partly with a new and dreadful sense of how important it was to keep her secret.

Where would she take Gregor to get well? To Grandmother Hoop? Would she help them? What about his own parents?

Annie considered these questions with half a mind; the other half she focused on two objectives: stay clear of the roving circles of torchlight that would reveal her to the men working the night shift and find a weapon. A club or a knife would do, but what she really needed was a pistol. They wouldn't keep them anywhere near the miners' tents. She skirted those, her ears, which seemed sharp tonight, picking up snores, a hacking cough, someone trying to swallow sobs. Her nose, too, was hard at work: wood smoke from the kiln; the usual men-smells of sweat and feet; damp wool; something burnt lingering from dinner; and that tinny sweetness that hung over everything here. Chopper smelled of it, Hauler smelled of it, even Gregor. The fruit she'd stolen from Chopper's garden had tasted of it, she realized, and had the funny sensation of feeling her mouth water and her stomach turn at the same time.

Annie stopped when she reached the tents where Gibbet's men slept. These were in better condition than those of the miners. They had wooden sides and stilts to keep them above the frost and mud. A lantern was lit in one of them and she could see two men in profile, one sitting, the other standing in front of him. The standing man was unwinding a piece of cloth from around the sitting man's head. She crept closer.

"Hurts!" said a muffled voice.

"Hold still, this will be the worst of it. There."

"How's it look?"

No answer.

"It looks bad?"

"It looks bad, Pip."

"Will I lose my eye?" the seated man asked in a small voice.

"Might do. Can't say. A scar though, definite."

"Like Chopper?"

The standing man chuckled. "Just like that, Pip. Terrify the orphans, for certain."

"Why'd he do it, Rube? It was just a slip. Just a little slip."

"You never call him that. Never. Not until he really is."

"King?" Pip whispered.

"Quiet! You want me to take your tongue, too?"

"Sorry, Rube. Sorry. But Rube?"

"What?"

"Where does he go all the time? What does he do?"

"He stays at Chopper's farm, you know that. Or sometimes"—here Rube's voice changed, and Annie could not tell if it was contempt, or surprise, or something else he was trying to suppress—"I heard sometimes he stays with his mother."

"But what does he *do*?"

"Sit still. I'm going to wrap you back up."

They were quiet for a few minutes except for an occasional whimper from Pip. Annie had just decided to continue her search for weapons when Rube spoke.

"They'll have a job for you, I think. A bad job."

"What?" Pip's voice was muffled again.

"A new chipper in today. Strong, and Hauler says Chopper caught her on the ladder in full dark, so either brave or dumb. We hope dumb." He chuckled. "Anyway, the beds are getting tight. And there's a runout."

"Aw, not that, Rube. I'm not the man for that."

"You're not the man for anything if you don't show them

you know how to keep quiet. Tough and quiet, like I always tell you, Pip. Tough and quiet."

A pause.

"How do I do it?"

"However you like, just so there's no trace."

"When?"

"The runout's in there now, all alone. Or maybe the new one is with him, but that's no matter. Just do it before the rest get off shift. And before Hauler wakes up. He doesn't like to know."

❧

"Gregor! Gregor, wake up."

Again and again she had to remind herself, as he stumbled and clung to her, that he was sick, that he couldn't see. But she wanted to shake him, to yell at him, *hurry, hurry, hurry*.

"Annie, stop. I can't. I can't."

He was panting, his arm around her neck, hers gripping his waist. She could feel his ribs through his back.

"Boots?" she asked.

"No boots. All burnt."

"Never mind."

Somehow, she got him through the door, a few feet down the path toward the cliff. Lights bobbed along the cliff top. Would the children carry lanterns? Would they chip blind?

She was nearly carrying him now. A wagon. If they could get to a wagon . . . there must be horses stabled somewhere. *Think, Annie, think.*

"Gregor, take this. Take a sip."

"From Grandmother Hoop?" he gasped.

"Yes." She closed his fingers around the vial.

"Yes," he said. "Yes."

"No, my kiddies. I'm afraid, no."

❧

Smirch stood with his hands on his hips and his head cocked to one side. His mouth was smug. A moment later Pip appeared, his head swaddled in bandages, and behind him a man Annie guessed to be Rube, holding a torch.

"You two take the runout. I'll take the girl. Bold as brass, this one." He shook his head. "Chopper liked you."

Annie tightened her arm around Gregor. Rube nodded at Pip, who took a step toward them. Smirch put his hand on her shoulder.

If Annie had had time to think, she wouldn't have done it. Of course she wouldn't have done it, something so strange. But she didn't think. She bit Smirch's hand, bit him so hard that blood spurted into her mouth and he screamed a thin scream of real pain.

Then, a blur. Running, Gregor running with her, a surge of hope—they were free!—and then a feeling of being cut in two, cold air where his body had touched hers. A pair of strong hands grabbed her under the arms, wrenching her upward. It was a mistake, lifting her like that. It left her feet free to kick, her hands free to punch and claw. Whoever was holding her let go, and she turned, frantic.

"Gregor!"

Something heavy and salt-smelling closed around her throat. "Too fresh," said a voice in her ear.

"Don't," she gasped.

He eased up, just a bit. "Don't what?"

"Don't let them toss him over. Don't."

Hauler stilled. "We'll see."

Then he flexed the arm around her throat, and a darkness fell that she could not see through.

Chapter 6

She woke in the pit on Chopper's farm. Her throat hurt. Her feet were cold. No boots. No Gregor. No cats.

She remembered certain things, like remembering a dream: jostling cart wheels, raised voices, the brightness of sunlight, a man's voice, "Kill her . . . Gibbet . . . wait . . . unusual," then a hand pinching her jaw and an awful sweetness filling her mouth. She could taste it still, the same sweetness that flavored everything here—the fruit she had stolen, the water Chopper had given her—but much stronger. The stiffness in her limbs told her she had been unconscious for many hours.

It took a moment to register that she was not alone in the pit. There was a rat. Her first thought was food. But then, as she watched, the rat sallied past her with a bit of old melon rind in its teeth, reached the side of pit, and disappeared.

Before, the pit had been shaped something like a teardrop: round on the sides and narrowed at the top, where the door was. Standing in the middle with her arms stretched out, her fingers had not quite reached any of the walls. Now she could flatten her palm against the side where the rat had disappeared. She crouched down. Bits of straw edged the rat hole. This was a wall, a mud wall. Someone had built this wall, and recently. Annie wiggled her fingers into the hole and tugged. A clump of dirt fell away.

Annie kicked the wall. *Smirch*. Kicked it again. *Chopper*. Kick. *Pip*. Kick. *Rube*. A very hard couple of kicks. *Gibbet*. *Uncle Jock*. She hesitated, foot raised. Should she kick Hauler?

Past the rubble of wall a room appeared, the mirror image of the pit. Except this room was full of ringstone: stone banked like snow against the walls, stone laid inches thick along the ground. Annie dropped to her knees. There were coins, too, some in the lesser currency of Howland, some she did not recognize. Big reddish coins stamped with the image of a bird. Heavy gray coins covered in strange symbols. Smooth, milky green coins that looked like buttons. She put one of each kind of foreign coin in her pocket, along with a handful of ringstone. A handful of white stone. It made her feel sick.

But now: a trail of rat droppings led her from the room into a low tunnel. She crawled a few yards and then dropped to her belly. The dirt around her smelled damp and alive, as though freshly turned over. Roots tickled her scalp. Then, as quickly as it had narrowed, the tunnel broadened, high and wide enough that a grown man could walk upright. From time to time she'd pass a burnt match or drops of hardened wax. After a mile or so the tunnel began to slope downward, so steeply in places she had to scoot on her backside. She'd come two miles at least. How long had it taken them to dig such a tunnel? Maybe not so very long, if you had arms like Hauler's.

Gradually she became aware of a strange sound, a sort of muted roar. The tunnel turned a sharp corner and she felt cold, delicious wind in her face. She had reached the river.

The air was still, tasting of night. A wooden dock led from the mouth of the tunnel to a muddy beach. A pair of rowboats had been tied to the dock. One held shovels and buckets, the other a few cooking utensils and a bag of oat flour.

For superior oatcakes use a very hot pan spread liberally with pork fat. Annie wondered what *The Book of Household Virtues* would make of her wet gobs of raw oats, washed down with moss-flavored river water.

At the highest part of the bank, stacked in a shallow dugout, were dozens of wooden crates. They were all the same, three feet long by two feet deep, with metal fastenings. They were all locked.

She walked a short ways south to where the river split itself on a grouping of boulders, spreading into a formation called Witch's Hand before drawing together again between the sheer rock cliffs of Dour Gorge. Gregor's father had fished Witch's Hand and made a small living. Then the notices went up.

WEST RIVER
SOUTH BORDER DOUR COUNTY TO BAY
TO BE HEREBY INCORPORATED WITH DOUR GORGE
AS PERTAINS TO ALL RIGHTS AND ACCESSES
BY ROYAL DECREE

Annie remembered reading the black lettering over and over with Gregor, uncertain what the words meant, certain they meant something important. With fishing off-limits, Gregor's father had tried farming, but then the farms had failed, all at once. Uncle Jock had come stamping into the house one afternoon, his hands and boots covered in sticky black dirt.

"Like poison, Primrose. Like planting in a bed of poison."

Aunt Prim had fetched him a whisky and said nothing about the dirt on the floor. The next summer, Gregor's parents sold him to the Dropmen.

Annie returned to the dock, stepping from rock to rock so as not to leave footprints. The tunnel connected to the smallest stream in the Witch's Hand, the pinkie finger. Though now a sluggish trickle, in spring the water would run high and fast.

"And cold. That whitewater will freeze you quicker than drown you. Keep to the bay, you pair." Gregor's father had looked at them sternly, then mussed their hair. Whatever Gibbet wanted to do with those crates and that ringstone, she thought he'd better finish before the river rose.

And then, just like that, Annie knew what to do. Knowing felt so much better than not knowing that even though her feet had frozen into icy lumps and a much worse lump of uncooked oats had balled in her stomach and she was alone, completely alone in the whole world, she smiled.

❦

It was early yet for a traveler to be on the roads. That the woman was a giant, at least as big as Hauler and considerably rounder, might have explained her boldness. And the yelling—perhaps the yelling was intended to scare off the kinder-stalk?

"HEY! Lo non-NEY! A lit-tle boy so bon-NEY! Came to me a courtin', at the sum-mer FAIR!"

Not yelling, Annie realized. Singing.

"He WORE a vest of sa-tin green, and britches vel-vet BROWN, a ring upon his finger, and flowers in his HAIR! And flow-ers in his HA-IR!"

Annie covered her ears on the final note. From her hiding place, she watched the wagon slow as it reached the cross-roads. A weathered wooden marker like a leafless tree pointed the four directions: west to the sea, north to the forest, south to the swamp, east to the city. The woman yawned, stretched, flexed her hands, had a drink of water, said something to the horse. *Go east*, Annie willed her. *East, east, east.*

"HEY! Lo non-NEY!"

East it was. With the road so full of rocks and ruts, the woman didn't seem to notice the slight lurch as Annie climbed aboard.

The wagon bed was full of junk: dirty straw, a couple of wilted cabbages, a crate filled with a jumble of metal parts: nails, screws, springs, a coil of delicate copper wire, a sheaf of silver beaten flat as paper. There was also, thankfully, an old blanket wrapped around some eggs. It was flecked with straw and none too clean, but Annie curled up under it, careful not to squash the eggs, and made herself as comfortable as she could.

The landscape changed as they traveled east. The bare

fields of Dour County gave way to fields of wheat, barley, and clover. Frilly curtains showed at the windows of houses. Wild primrose grew along the roadside. After a time they turned south and the houses clustered together into towns. They passed a school where children milled around the front gate. They passed a haberdashery, a print shop, a bakery with yellow cakes cooling on trays by the open window. When they stopped for the night at a public house, Annie lay still as a corpse until the driver had locked horse and wagon into the barn and her heavy footsteps had carried her to the inn. The barn was quiet and warm and full of animal smells. Unable to help herself, Annie ate a couple of eggs. They tasted of nothing but wetness.

Then she slept, a deep, dreamless sleep, waking only briefly when the barn doors opened at dawn. She slept through miles of road. She slept even after the wagon had jolted to a stop, even after the driver had climbed down and made her way to the back.

"By my mother's best silk stockings! Who are you?"

Annie woke and looked up into a face with cheeks the color of cooked beets. Standing over her was the tallest, broadest, bosomiest person she had ever seen. The woman held an egg in each hand, ready to pelt her if she turned out to be dangerous.

"I'm sorry," Annie croaked. "I was going east, and I thought if you were, too . . . I can pay my way if you like. I have plenty of money."

The woman's face fell out of its astonished expression into a warm, wrinkly smile.

"Now, now, you can ride in my wagon any time you want, only you'll have to sit up front and keep me company next time. Poor thing." She reached to pick a piece of straw from Annie's hair. Annie flinched, and the woman's face became wrinklier than ever.

"Oh, you poor little gal. Come along and meet Bea—that's my sister—and oh, where are my manners? My name is Serena. Serena Verbena, if you can believe it. Anyhow, we'll get settled and fry some eggs and then have a snooze. Day after tomorrow I'm on to Magnifica, if you're going that far, but tonight, thank goodness, I can sleep in my own bed."

Dazed, Annie followed the enormous woman through a tiny gate into a tiny yard bordering a tiny cottage. Serena bent over almost double to fit through the door. Inside, the ginger-colored bun on the top of her head was flattened against the ceiling. Everything was painted light blue or cherry red or lemon yellow, from the rafters in the low ceiling to the rungs of the miniature chairs. One of the chairs, a bright red rocker, looked at least three times as big as the others.

"Beatrice! I have arrived!"

A woman appeared in the kitchen doorway, holding out her arms and smiling. "Serena, back at last."

Beatrice was a perfect replica of her sister; only where Serena was very large, Beatrice was exceptionally small, down to the tiny ginger bun perched on top of her head. Serena stepped forward to embrace her sister and for a moment Annie thought she would take the roof of the cottage with her. There was not the slightest speck of dirt anywhere in the cottage, but in every corner of every rafter was a spiderweb, and in every web, a fat spider. Some of the spiders were gold and brown, some were black and red, others were beige with green and rose bellies.

"Welcome to our home. I see you've noticed the ladies." Beatrice spoke gently, but Annie blushed, ashamed to have been caught staring.

"That's perfectly all right, dear. Most people think it's a bit odd. I'm a weaver, you see." She gestured toward a diminutive loom in one corner of the room. "Once or twice a day, I stand up on a chair and have a good close look at one of the webs. Each has her own style, and they aren't afraid to experiment. Besides, they eat mosquitoes, and if there's one thing I hate in this world it's the whine of a mosquito." She paused and looked at Annie more closely.

"What on earth am I going on about? This child is dead on her feet. Serena, get the tub. Young lady, sit down. Now what would you like for dinner? We've got eggs and cheese and some decent bread—a *bit* hard, but only at the heel, and that's all right if you want to make frogs-in-a-hole . . ." Her voice trailed off. Both sisters looked at Annie expectantly. To her horror, Annie began to cry—not just trickles, but huge sobs, as if she would actually heave her heart out of her chest and onto the floor.

The next thing she knew, she was in Serena's lap in the rocking chair. By the time Annie's sobs had subsided to hiccups, the front of Serena's dress was soaked through. Beatrice had been out and back to tend to the horse, and night had fallen, swift as ever, outside the windows. Annie peeked up at

Serena. The woman returned her gaze without a hint of embarrassment. Then she stood, as indifferent to Annie's weight as if she really were a baby, and gently placed Annie back down in the chair.

"Bea, we'd better make some tea. There can't be a drop of water left in this child's body."

The women disappeared into the kitchen. Soon Annie heard the clatter of pots, then the delicious smell of eggs frying. Snatches of their conversation drifted out to her.

"Who are her people? . . . Must have jumped in outside Gorgetown . . . stocking-feet! Did you see . . . a dark sign . . . nonsense, Serena."

Annie leaned back and let the words pass over her. The cushions on all the chairs were covered with intricate flower designs, petals overlapping petals until they blended together into swirls of color. Annie held one of the pillows in her lap to study it. You wouldn't notice it the first or even the second time you looked, but in the midst of the flowers Beatrice had sewn a pair of eyes and the pointed, watchful face of a cat. The cat seemed to be hiding somehow behind the pillow, waiting to pounce. Annie couldn't help turning the pillow over, but of course there was just the plain fabric backing. She traced the stripes on the cat's face with her finger.

"Ah, you've spotted him." Beatrice set down the tray she was carrying and came over to Annie. "That's Sunshine Maxmillian Beaugriffe."

"Beaugriffe Maxmillian Sunshine!" Serena hollered from the kitchen.

Bea rolled her eyes. "There may have been a small dispute during the naming process. Not everyone notices him in there, you know. Only people who love cats." She frowned. "Or perhaps embroidery. Or I suppose a person could love both cats *and* embroidery."

"Is he still here?" Annie asked, looking around hopefully.

"Oh no, dear. Sunny lived with us for nineteen years and spent every minute of his life asleep on that chair."

"Asleep on that chair or in my foxgloves—or rather, on my foxgloves," Serena said, and set down an immense wooden tub in the middle of the room.

"Do you have a pet?" Bea asked politely.

"I, they weren't . . . but I had, I did . . ." Annie felt ready to cry again.

"Oh my dear child!" said the sisters in unison. Bea took Annie's hand in hers. "Tell us. What is your name, and how is it that you are so alone?"

Annie looked at their faces with their duplicate expressions of concern and felt a sudden urge to tell them everything. She struggled with herself for a moment, then said simply, "My name is Annie. I have a message for the king, and I'm going to the palace to give it to him."

The women exchanged a glance. Annie couldn't blame them. Standing on the riverbank, her plan had made perfect sense: tell the king that Gibbet's men were stealing from the Drop and the king would arrest the men, close the mine, and rescue Gregor. Spoken aloud, the words sounded worse than ridiculous.

The twins were conferring in whispers. Bea opened her hand to show two white ringstones. Annie had left them in place of the eggs.

"Are these yours, dear?"

Annie shook her head. "They're yours. My fare, for the trip. Room and board."

Serena started to say something, but Annie cut her off. "I have plenty. Look."

She reached into her pocket and drew out a fistful of the stones. Bea made a strangled sound and turned away. Serena, pale, her hand trembling, pressed Annie's fingers closed over the heap of ringstone.

"I don't want to see those again in this house. But you stay here with us and have something good to eat, and then I'll take you east, as far as Magnifica. Bea, give the stones back."

"No! They're for you."

"We could not ... stones like these are ...," Serena began, but Beatrice frowned at her.

"Very well. These two we will keep. Now, for pity's sake, let's eat."

Annie ate and ate and ate. She ate more than Serena, who was trying to reduce, and more than Beatrice, who was trying to plump. When she had finished her eggs, Beatrice fed her bread pudding and milky, sugary tea. Finally, Annie set down her fork. She yawned.

"A bath, then bed," Beatrice said decisively.

While Beatrice brushed the tangles out of Annie's hair, Serena emptied kettleful after kettleful of steaming water into the tub. She mixed in salts and a powder that smelled of rose-mary. The steam from the bath and the soft tugging of the hairbrush made Annie drowsy. She had just nodded off when she heard Beatrice give a little gasp, then try to cover the sound with a cough.

"What is it?" Annie asked, alarmed.

"Oh, I'm so silly. It's only—were you hurt? I've heard that white hair will sometimes grow from a wound . . ." She trailed off, embarrassed.

Annie turned to face her. "I don't know what you mean."

Beatrice studied Annie for a moment. Her own face relaxed. "Let me show you."

She got up and disappeared into her bedroom. When she returned, she was holding two small silver-backed mirrors. One of them she handed to Annie.

"You hold this, yes, just like that, and I'll hold the other. Now, keep still." She took hold of Annie's hair with her free hand and wrapped it around her wrist, lifting the mass so that the back of Annie's neck was bare. There, just at her nape, was a thick streak of white. It wasn't ugly, exactly, just . . . strange. Annie peered into the mirror, trying to get a better look.

"I don't know where that's from. I've never seen it before, but that's not a place I usually look." She giggled a bit at this, and Beatrice giggled too.

"No, I suppose you wouldn't."

The sisters retreated to the kitchen while Annie bathed. Annie was grateful for the privacy, not because she was shy, but because of the mortifying layer of grime that collected on the surface of the water even before she began to scrub. When she was finished, Beatrice brought her one of her own clean nightgowns and combed out her hair a second time.

At last Beatrice led Annie to a tiny room under the eaves. It reminded Annie of the garret, except this room had a neat little bed and dresser and white curtains drawn tight against the darkness.

Bea had offered to wash her dress, but Annie refused. Now she found it carefully folded at the foot of the bed. The bed was covered by a quilt woven with a pattern of flying birds. Among the birds Annie placed the lock of blond hair, the white ringstone she had stolen from Uncle Jock, the rock she had meant as a gift for Gregor, and Page's book. The two handfuls of ringstone from the pit she set slightly apart. They were not as brilliant as the stone Gibbet had given Uncle Jock, and opaque where that stone was almost translucent. What would they buy? A palace? A city? These were her treasures, but there was something awful about each of them. Quickly she hid everything again in her dress.

That night she dreamt of birds. A crowd of ravens sparring with a hawk. The red bird separated from the rest and flew toward the forest.

Scritch, scritch.

A bird was at the window, knocking at the glass with its beak.

Scritch, scritch.

Two birds, scratching the glass with their talons.

Annie realized that she was awake, the birds flocking on

the quilt set in motion by the flicker of the candle at her bed-side.

Scritch, scritch, scritch.

The sound was not angry, or even impatient, just persistent. And—Annie sat up straight—familiar.

She opened the window, just a crack, and immediately felt pressure on the other side, pushing it wider. And then there he was, his big square head followed by the whole long length of him. Close on Izzy's heels, so close that their bodies overlapped, orange and brown, brown and orange, came Prudence.

Chapter 7

The twins were beside themselves over the cats. Serena fed all three of them milk and eggs for breakfast, and Bea offered to comb their fur as she had Annie's hair. Of course Izzy would have nothing to do with it, but Prudence sat politely for a few strokes. She looked ragged and lean and a little wild. Where had they been?

The day passed peacefully. Serena locked herself in a room she called "the magic shop" at the back of the house. Occasional clanks and screeches issued from behind the closed door, and twice Annie heard what she could have sworn was a rooster. When Serena emerged for lunch her fingers were coated with silver dust.

Annie sat on a cushion on the floor, helping Beatrice wind spools of thread.

"This is the ninth shade of green! How do you remember all the names?"

"Oh I don't, dear. I used to try, because it seemed like fun, naming them all." She held up a spool of dingy white thread.

"This might be 'bone,' but then what's this? 'Bleached bone'? and this? 'Jaundiced bone'?"

Annie giggled.

"Needless to say I got tired of that pretty quick. Now it's just green-one, green-two, and so on. Serena can tell you how I run around the house calling, 'Where's my pink-54? Where's my yellow-99?'"

"Will you be coming to Magnifica with us?" Annie asked shyly.

"I'm afraid not, dear. It's Serena who likes to go traipsing around the countryside. Can't stand the thought she might miss something, a market, a festival." She laughed and waved her hand around the room. "Not much happens here, so who can blame her? But I like it. In any case, it would take a good deal more than Magnifica to get me out of these." She wiggled her toes in their embroidered slippers. Serena had a similar pair: blue instead of green and twice as large.

"Don't you like it there?"

"Oh, it's silly I suppose, after all this time, but I can't help thinking of the miners."

Annie's breath caught in a hiccup. "Miners?"

"No one's ever told you about the mine? About how Magnifica came to be?"

Annie shook her head.

"Well, it's not a nice story, dear. Do you want to hear it? Yes? Very well."

Beatrice began to work the pedal of the loom with her foot, her voice blending with its gentle whir.

"Not long after ringstone was first discovered in Howland, a group of prospectors traveled west to see what they could find. They made their camp, and in the morning each man set out in a different direction. Among them was a man named Terrance Uncton. As he walked along, Uncton stumbled over a rock poking through the dirt. On the rock was a round, shiny patch of ringstone, gleaming like the skin on a bald man's head.

"At first he thought it no great find, a few inches of ringstone at most, enough for a belt buckle or perhaps a serving dish. But as he cut into the rock he discovered that the shiny patch was only the top of a column that extended far underground. For weeks Uncton kept his discovery a secret, but as he dug farther, the column grew thicker. When it reached the thickness of a man's body, Uncton realized he would need help. But first, with his sharpest chisel, he carved the words 'Prop. of Tr. Uncton' into the top of the column.

"The prospectors followed the column down, twenty, fifty, a hundred, then two hundred feet deep, until they came to the ringstone's mighty root. They broadened the mine and built entrances and exits, pulley systems and trusses. They built an entire underground network of catwalks and tunnels along which the miners could travel for days without ever coming to the surface.

"So much dust blew up from the bottom of the mine that nothing grew for a quarter mile in every direction from the mine's entrance. Barracks sprang up to house the miners, and it was not unusual for a child to come in after playing outdoors covered with yellow dust. The prospectors and their families settled around the mine and grew rich, though none more than Terrance Uncton. From there the city grew.

"The ringstone in the mine lasted a long time, but as the column was cut closer and closer to its base, getting at the stone eventually came to be more trouble than it was worth. The air at the bottom of the mine was thin and the ringstone harder and more difficult to cut. At last only the poorest men ventured down. They breathed air through hoses threaded down the mineshaft and scraped at the stone with homemade chisels, often staying below ground for weeks at a time. When a miner had collected enough ringstone to satisfy him he blew three times on the whistle he wore around his neck. A man waiting at the top would turn the great wheel to which the miner's waist-rope was attached and haul the miner to the surface. Before he left the mine, the miner paid thirty percent of his take to the man who hauled him up.

"One day the mine collapsed in on itself. A hundred years' worth of trusses, rigging, planks, wheelbarrows, spades, hoses, dirt, and rubble fell into the hole, burying the miners at the bottom and closing the mine for good. Above the roar of falling earth the man at the mine entrance heard the shrilling of dozens of whistles. Then the earth moved beneath him and he, too, along with his wheel, disappeared into the hole."

Beatrice fell quiet, and for a long time the only sound was the whir of the spinning wheel. Then that faded, and Annie looked up to find Beatrice watching her.

"Can you still visit the mine?" Annie asked, feeling she should say something.

Beatrice gave an odd smile. "Of course not, dear. That's where they've built the palace."

❧

They rose at dawn the next morning. Bea was the sort of person who always looked wide-awake, but Serena . . .

"Tea, Beatrice!"

Beatrice handed her sister a cup of hot tea. Serena swallowed the tea in one gulp and held out the empty cup. "Tea, Beatrice!"

Beatrice filled, Serena swallowed, and so on. Six times.

Serena set down her cup. "Thank you, Beatrice."

"You are most welcome, Serena."

"Annie, gather your felines. We are off!"

Beatrice followed them into the yard. It was colder than the day before and the air felt sharp. Annie sniffed. "It will snow soon."

"Yes, you two—get going. There are extra blankets in the back, and a canvas if it gets really wet. And mother's pistol."

"Mother's pistol?" Serena raised her eyebrows.

"For Annie. In the event that . . . should anything . . ."

"Beatrice."

"Oh, I didn't want to worry you! It could very well be hogwash, and you know how people love to spread trouble, and it being Annie's first trip . . ."

"*Beatrice!*"

Bea looked uncertainly at Annie. "Perhaps Annie should . . ."

"Bea. I believe our Annie is more than equal to hearing a little talk of"—she looked hard at her sister—"kinderstalk, is it?"

Bea nodded. "A man traveling outside of Balesville saw them. Day before yesterday."

"Balesville! Why, that's in Broad County! We passed through there on our way home!"

"I know," Bea said unhappily.

"How many?"

"Three, just sitting by the side of the road plain as day. What that fellow must have thought! His horse bolted before he could take any kind of aim, but the funny thing is they didn't give chase. They just sat there, he said. Watching."

"Who told you this?"

Beatrice blushed. "Claire Fauxall. I ran into her at market. It's why I didn't tell you before."

Serena looked cross, but she also looked worried. "If even a grain of it's true . . . But I'll bet Annie knows her way around a pistol, yes?"

"Yes." Annie was disgusted by how small her voice sounded.

"Now don't you worry! It's just a precaution. I've got Dad's old fowler under the seat, and I'm a better shot than he was."

"I should hope so," Bea murmured, and the sisters snickered.

"Broad County is quite far from the forest, isn't it?" Annie said. "Nearly as far as we are here?"

"We haven't had a kinderstalk sighting in years, and now this. I don't suppose you brought them with you?"

"Serena! That's not funny."

"Well! I was only trying to lighten the mood."

"When did you ever hear a good joke about kinderstalk?"

As casually as possible Annie said, "I'd like to borrow a hat, please. Or a wig, if you have one, or . . . or anything, really, to cover my head and my . . . my face."

The sisters stopped bickering and stared at her.

"Annie, do you know how to bridle a horse?" Beatrice asked. "Perhaps you could do that now, to save us some time?"

Annie slipped away to the small outbuilding the sisters used for a barn. She looked back and saw them huddled in conference, Serena gesticulating, Bea with hands on her hips.

There was only the one horse inside, chewing his oats.

"Hello, horse," Annie said quietly.

When Annie returned from the barn, Beatrice was standing by the wagon holding a wig of floppy orange ringlets.

"Here." She handed the wig to Annie. "This was Mother's. She never liked anyone to know that her hair had . . . how shall we say?" She glanced at her sister and suppressed a smile. "Fallen clean out."

Beatrice hovered around Annie and Serena as they finished packing the wagon, tightening what was already tight, neatening what was already straight.

Serena turned to her sister. "Good-bye, darling Bea."

"Good-bye, precious Serena." This time it was Beatrice, tiny as she was, who seemed to engulf her sister. "Come back directly, once you've made the delivery. No dawdling."

"Now, Bea, have you ever known me to dawdle?" Serena

climbed onto the wagon seat and sat down heavily. Beatrice settled the wig on Annie's head, tucking up her long dark hair.

"Wait. I have something else for you. I had to guess the size, and there wasn't time for . . . the faces aren't as detailed as I'd like, but I think I've . . . Perhaps you can wear them until you get proper boots." She shrugged and blushed.

The slippers had peaked toes and stiff leather soles that must have taken hours to sew on. Against a crimson background Bea had stitched two cat faces: Prudence on the right foot, with her wide eyes and sweetness, and Izzy on the left, his ear torn, his expression imperious.

They fit perfectly.

Annie felt something old stir inside her, something she had not felt even with Page—not a memory exactly, but something warm and safe, something of her mother.

She did not know what to say. She held Bea's hand. Bea's palm was soft but each of her fingers had a callus at the tip from working the loom.

"Good luck, Annie. You will always be welcome here."

Serena drove while Annie studied the map. Serena hardly needed directions to Magnifica, but Annie enjoyed plotting their course.

"Which way at the turning now?"

"Go right, then the road forks again. Jog left, then straight, then right again at the stone cross."

"Right! Left! Straight! Right again! Whoever heard of such a silly road!"

The cats perched on the seat between them, staring straight ahead like a pair of figureheads. Far to the north Annie could make out a dark shape she thought must be the forest. Were the kinderstalk hunting during the day now? Were the sightings real? She thought of Gibbet and his sack of rabbits. She thought of the kinderstalk standing on its hind legs, like a man.

The air continued to grow colder, and though there were no clouds the sky looked washed out, the sun a pale orb. Annie felt a weight press heavily against her left shoulder. Serena had dozed off and was listing to one side like a boat threatening to capsize.

The horse, sensing that his driver's attention was elsewhere, stood stock-still in the middle of the road.

"Serena, uh, could you . . ." Annie's voice trailed off. They had come to a stop perhaps twenty feet from the stone cross that pointed toward Magnifica. The road, where they had only recently passed booksellers, junkmen, even a cartload of acrobats, was deserted.

She saw the tail first, a thick black plume, as the creature stood, stretched, and stepped from behind the cross. It looked both better and worse than she remembered: bigger, nearly as big as the horse, and terrifyingly out of place. But the face— there was expression in it. The honey-colored eyes met hers. Instinctively, Annie put her hand on Izzy's back, then lifted it away, startled. He was purring.

But the horse had begun to dance and roll his eyes. He

jerked a few steps sideways and the wagon jerked with him, tipping Serena upright. She looked at Annie sheepishly.

"Oh, my! I am sorry. I do enjoy a nap, at my age. Have I drooled on myself? Have I drooled on *yourself*?" She shook the reins. "And what's gotten into you, fellow? Eager for your oats, I'll bet. Hop to it, then. Which way, Annie? Which way at the cross?"

Annie stared behind her as they drove away. The kinder-stalk had disappeared, but she could not shake its image from her mind, the fur coal black except for a diamond-shaped patch of white on the breast.

As the hours stretched themselves out, Serena told Annie about her previous trips to Magnifica. Unlike Bea, she loved the city, with its crowds and shops and sparkling white stone buildings. And the palace! Each of the mullioned windows was shaped differently, with every pane a different color of glass. The doors to the palace were solid brass with ringstone inlay, weighing several tons apiece. Serena visited Magnifica two or three times a year to deliver goods and stock up on the parts she couldn't buy locally. Where Bea had become a weaver like their mother, Serena had taken up their father's trade.

"Most of what I do is humdrum repairs around the village, but every so often I get a specialty order from the city. Reach under the seat there, Annie. I'll show you what I mean."

Annie pulled out a lumpy bundle wrapped in sackcloth.

It was about the length of her arm, but not heavy. Annie hesitated.

"Go on, open it."

Inside the sackcloth was a smaller bundle wrapped in soft flannel, and inside that an even smaller bundle wrapped in rose-colored satin. Annie felt strangely nervous as she unwrapped the final covering. Resting among the folds of satin, as if inside a luxurious coffin, was a mechanical man. He was made of hammered silver and, though barely a foot long, precise in every detail: his neck moved so he could turn his head; his knees and elbows bent; his eyelids lifted up and down so he looked alternately startled, crafty, and asleep; each delicate finger was perfectly articulated, the three joints made out of tiny loops of silver wire.

But it was his heart from which Annie could not look away. There, in the center of his chest, Serena had placed the clock itself. She had built it in the shape of a heart—not a valentine but a real human heart, with four chambers, minute ventricles, and the clasps that held the clock in place cunningly shaped to look like arteries. It was the size of a human heart, much too big for the miniature body, but still somehow perfect. The heart ticked steadily. Annie stared at Serena. She felt afraid—not of Serena, but of something.

Her voice came out a hoarse whisper. "You made this?"

Serena had been looking at Annie oddly, but now she smiled.

"Yes. He keeps perfect time, too, with no winding. It will be painful to part with him; he's been a part of my life for so long now. Two years he's taken! But I always knew this day would come, and considering *who* . . ." She paused and gave Annie a cunning look. "Can you tell me who it's for?"

Annie studied the clock again. She had been so struck by the heart that she hadn't noticed the gold crown, studded with tiny chips of ringstone, the papery ruffles on the breeches, the stiff collar of silver beaten so thin it was almost translucent.

"He's the . . . it's the king."

"Indeed! The king himself. It's very flattering to be asked, naturally. I *do* have something of a reputation in the city. He even had me summoned to the palace. I didn't go *inside*, of course. I only hope he likes it. He wanted something in his own image, something unique, 'a thing no one else had yet dreamt of.' Those were his precise words. Imagine! An order like that, after so many years of cuckoo clocks!"

Serena had been speaking too loudly, too cheerfully, perhaps to compensate for Annie's silence. Now her voice faltered.

"I did hesitate at first—such responsibility! But I'll never have to work again, Annie, I mean the repairs, the routine business. I'll be able to concentrate on the"—she blushed—"on the art."

"It *is* art," Annie said. "It's astonishing. And it's so . . . so *anatomical*." Page had shown her drawings from one of their parents' books, the body without skin, showing all the muscles, and another showing just the organs. Everything had seemed awfully crowded together. Serena blushed again, but she looked pleased.

"Well, I did spend a year at the Royal Institute of Medicine. They don't usually allow women, you know. Beatrice always says she was born to be a weaver, but I . . . well, in any event, I couldn't stay once Mother and Dad died. Though I must say it comes in handy when one of us gets a splinter or some little thing." She looked at the clock, her expression wistful. "Now wrap him back up. We don't want any dust in the works."

They drove on a while in silence. Annie wanted to unwrap the clock again and look at it, but it also made her uneasy, as though there were another person in the wagon with them. Suddenly she sat up straight.

"Serena! Are we going to the palace to deliver the clock?"

"Oh no, dear, no one simply *goes* to the palace. Once we arrive at the inn, we'll send word that the order has arrived, then wait to be summoned. Then, once we're summoned, we'll drive to the bottom of that big hill the palace is built on and wait to be summoned again. He's very secretive, our king. I've even heard"—she lowered her voice—"it's rumored that if anyone speaks of what happens inside the palace to someone on the outside, he, well, he loses his tongue. I mean it's actually cut off. There's supposed to be someone in the king's service whose sole duty it is to cut out tongues. But well, honestly, that does seem unlikely, doesn't it?"

Annie tried to smile, but her lips felt stuck to her teeth.

Traffic from the city had started to clog the roadway. Workhorses rubbed shoulders with courtiers' mounts. A wagon full of turnips was forced into the ditch by a carriage as white and round as an egg. Gold velvet curtains fluttered at the window as the horses charged past.

"Ridiculous, with their new-bought names," Serena muttered, but Annie was watching a sheep farmer hustle his flock across the road. A black and white dog nipped and nudged the sheep along. Annie thought of the kinderstalk she had seen in the road. There was no reason not tell Serena. In fact she *ought* to tell Serena. But she didn't.

Then, as they crested a hill the great city itself appeared, a shimmering white mass, with the palace perched above it like the top layer of a wedding cake.

"Looks good enough to eat, doesn't it?" said Serena.

Chapter 8

The inn was simple by Magnifica's standards, but far grander than any building in Dour County. As soon as they reserved a room Serena stumped off to investigate the kitchen, leaving Annie alone in the foyer with the innkeeper. She was a thin woman with a white starched collar that matched her teeth.

"What pretty red hair you have," the innkeeper said, and Annie knew immediately the wig looked a fright.

As she followed the innkeeper past the kitchen, Annie saw Serena sitting around a big table with the maids and stable boys. She was laughing and gesturing broadly with one hand; in the other she held a tankard filled with foamy ale. Annie hurried up the stairs.

The room was clean and impersonal, with a square bed in the center that looked big enough even for Serena. The innkeeper walked over to the window and twitched back the curtains. The sky was filled with pale, hazy light.

"You got here just in time. Snow is coming, our first big storm of the season. They say the roads will be impassable by morning." She all but smacked her lips with satisfaction, and Annie realized that if the guests were snowed in they would all have to pay for a second night.

"Is there anything I can get you?" she asked.

Annie shook her head and the woman left, closing the door smartly behind her.

The room looked out over the stables behind the inn. She could see Baggy, Serena's horse, munching hay with the other horses. Annie pressed her nose up against the glass. There was Izzy, an orange crescent on the floor of the stall, and Prudence, harder to distinguish from the matted hay, curled around him.

Annie sat cross-legged in the middle of the bed. Every time she opened Page's book she felt the same irrational burst of disappointment that the words hadn't magically resolved themselves into sense. But this time she saw something she had missed before. At the bottom of the paper Page had penciled a few lines, then rubbed them out. Annie squinted at the words: *The cion preserves its natural purity and intent, though it be fed and nourished by a mere crab.*

Below the quotation Page had written: *Scion? Fruit Trees? What mark? What!*

None of it made sense, but Annie liked the evidence of her sister's impatience. It made her seem alive.

❧

Serena, meanwhile, had challenged the stable boys to arm wrestling. She came up the stairs humming the strains of

Schragg's "Triumphal March" and opened the door with a flourish, brandishing a loaf of bread and a round of cheese.

"Behold! The spoils of— Child! What are you doing here in the dark?"

Annie raised her head and looked at Serena blankly.

"Child?" Serena's voice quavered.

Annie answered in a rush, fumbling and babbling.

"Serena, hello! It *has* gotten dark . . . must have dozed off . . . Sorry about the cold, I meant to call the maid. Let me get the . . ." But Serena had already crossed the room in a swish of skirts and ale fumes and yanked the curtains shut.

"Let's have some light then, anyway."

Warm light filled the room. Serena glanced at the book in Annie's lap. She opened her mouth, then shut it. She raised her fingers to her eyes and pressed them closed. Then she began to laugh, a big, shaking belly laugh.

"How Beatrice would chew my ear if she knew! Not the drinking. After such a long day on the road even she might take a drop. Still, that's no excuse." As she spoke she began to fumble with the buttons at the neck of her dress, then stopped in the middle to take off one shoe, then stumped around in her stocking foot because she decided she had better wash her face.

"They're all abuzz downstairs, Annie. The king's marriage this! The king's marriage that! There's a grand party tonight to formally introduce his betrothed to the court. A foundling they say, turned up at the palace gates these two years past, and now the king in love! Of course she's the picture of beauty. They've been carting food and frippery up the hill all week—even a cage of live peacocks, someone said! Oh!" Serena grinned through a mask of suds. "Do you think the clock is for his bride? A wedding gift? How romantic!"

Ghastly romantic, Annie thought, but she nodded and smiled. When Serena's back was turned she rolled to the side of the bed closer to the door and eased under the covers, fully dressed.

The bed gave a deep groan and Annie smiled despite herself at the sight of Serena swathed in yards of white nightgown—easily enough fabric for a full set of sails—her long red hair undone around her shoulders. She'd made a kind of poultice, smelling damply of chamomile and some stronger, more bitter herb, which she laid across her eyes.

"Keeps off the headache, no question." She reached out to pat Annie goodnight and nearly broke her nose.

She fell asleep like that, one arm across Annie's sternum like a lead weight, snoring so loudly that Annie half expected the innkeeper to come up and boot them both out into the snow.

Annie lay there thinking for a long time. She didn't know what to do. She knew what she *should* do, what she had been planning to do, but now that the opportunity had finally arrived—the perfect opportunity, really—she felt afraid. Not of what might happen to her, but of what would never happen. She would not wake up to Serena clucking about the snow. They would not play cards and eat warm dinners until the roads cleared. She would not try and fail to get an audience with the king. She would not return with Serena to the cottage.

The little room with the bird-patterned quilt would not be hers.

Annie squeezed her eyes shut, but it wasn't Serena laughing or Bea combing her hair that she saw. It was Gregor, with his old man's face and his child's body. She had to tell the king about Gibbet and the children at the Drop. She had to do it tonight.

Annie lifted Serena's arm from her chest. It took both hands to do it. She had no paper or ink to write a note, but she did have a hard cheese and a dull knife. "My thanks" she carved into the top of the cheese. Then she cut a big piece off the bottom and popped it into her mouth.

❧

The front door was heavily barred, but the bar wasn't as heavy as Serena's arm. The outside air hit her face, swept into her lungs, and made her ribs ache. Snow was falling thick and fast, brittle flakes that stuck to the fabric of her cloak like burrs. As she crossed the yard, her feet left dark prints that filled in with snow almost as soon as she made them.

The cats were waiting for her by the stable. Prudence waved her tail.

"Are you ready?" Annie whispered, more to herself than the cats. Isadore turned and trotted out of the yard. Annie couldn't help smiling at the familiar sight of his orange hindquarters bobbing along in front of her.

They followed the same road Serena had driven during the day, heading steadily east. The dark here was nothing like the dark of Dour County. Torches burned in every doorway. Lanterns hung on posts along the road. The firelight confused her. Could others see as well as she could? She hugged the ditch, the darkest part of the road, and stopped often, vainly, to listen. The white noise of falling snow swallowed every other sound.

Once inside the city proper, the road branched off a dozen times or more, each route marked with a sign. Annie's heart sped up when she saw the name of the road they were on: Royal Way.

Quite suddenly, the road flared into a semicircle and ended. No, it didn't end, exactly, just narrowed as it wound around the sides of the hill like a white ribbon. Serena had not exaggerated: the road was so narrow and the switchbacks so tight that only the lightest, nimblest carriages could navigate it. Tradespeople, unless they wanted to proceed on foot, would have to wait at the bottom for someone from the palace to come to them. When the snow cleared, Serena would be waiting here to deliver her clock.

They had taken three turns of the switchback and already Annie was out of breath. She counted fifteen more turns to the top.

"Izzy, slow—"

But he had already stopped. His ears stiffened. The tip of his tail flicked from side to side. An odd sound reached them. *Like Aunt Prim sifting flour*, Annie thought as she turned. Royal

Way stretched out below her with its dozens of small roads branching off. From every road, at every turning, kinderstalk appeared, until the avenue was filled with black bodies, all running toward her. Their feet sifted the snow, *shush, shush, shush.*

"Hurry!" Annie cried to the cats. "This way!"

But they didn't hurry. Only when Annie left the road to clamber up the rocky hillside did they follow her, and still they moved as if half-asleep.

Snow stung her bare hands. The rocks were all roughly the same shape and size, and she began to be familiar with their spacing—hand up, foot up, push with other hand, straighten leg. This wasn't a real hill at all, but man-made. She remembered what Beatrice had told her.

Can you still visit the mine?

Of course not, dear. That's where they've built the palace.

The kinderstalk were close now. She couldn't see them, couldn't afford to stop long enough to turn around, but she knew they were on the road. The shushing sound grew louder as they reached the turns nearest her, then faded as they followed the switchback in the other direction.

Finally, *finally*, she saw the sharp crest of the hill above her, and then, as she dragged herself up and over the edge, she saw something else: a pair of boots. With a gasp, Annie ducked back down. The guard, standing in a pool of torchlight, hadn't seen her. A match hit the snow near Annie's face and flared out. The guard inhaled deeply on his pipe, stamping his feet to bring feeling back to his toes. Snowflakes dusted his cap and the shoulders of his coat. *Couldn't he hear them? Couldn't he feel them coming?*

The guard stood in the lee of a stone arch, a high wall stretching away on either side of him. The gates were open, and getting around him was easy enough as long as she stayed out of the light. She hoped he would hear them in time, hoped his weapons might protect him, but she couldn't risk him stopping her.

When she was safely past, she cried a warning. "Kinderstalk!"

The kinderstalk poured over the edge of the plateau. The guard screamed. She ran faster, fast as an animal. Torches burned at intervals along the avenue. Annie burst into a pool of light, then burst back into the visible darkness as she ran toward the next light. She couldn't see the cats anymore; she couldn't see anything but the wavering lights lined up ahead of her. Somewhere beyond her were the palace doors. How much farther?

The kinderstalk pounded down the road after her. Now Annie could make out a second sound: panting. *Don't look back. Don't look back.*

She looked.

I am going to die, Annie thought.

Ahead of her were the gleaming brass and ringstone doors of the palace. Annie heard laughter, music, the tinkle of silverware against china. The party. And someone, drunk, happy, reckless, had left the doors open. This was just the kind of mistake she had been counting on, but not now, not with a hundred kinderstalk to follow her inside.

With the last of her breath, Annie screamed again, "Kinderstalk!" The word hung in the air for a moment, like the last, long note of a song.

Something cold and wet grazed the back of her hand, followed by hot breath where the coldness had been. She tried to jerk away, but there was tugging now at her cloak, at the hem of her dress. A weight pressed against her knees and she stumbled backward, her legs rising level with her body. For a moment she seemed to float.

Warm breath touched her skin again, this time at her neck. In a burst of panic, Annie fought her way upright and threw herself toward the doors. Her palms smacked cold brass. They had heard her in time. They had saved themselves.

They had left her to die.

Desperately, she pounded on the doors, and, though she refused to look, she felt the creatures around her, pressing against her, and smelled their sharp, wild scent—earth and blood, moss and pine.

"Help me!" she cried. "Help me! Help me! Help me!"

Help her! Help her! Help her!

A second voice joined hers, or seemed to, and then it was impossible to know, for the kinderstalk started to howl. The sound traveled like a shadow over the earth, back over the road, back past the inn, past Beatrice and Serena's house, back, back, back, all the long way she had traveled, back to Dour County and the very heart of the forest. The ground shifted under Annie's feet and she felt herself falling. *So this is what it is to die,* she thought. *I wonder if she is here.* Annie turned her head to look, and there, hovering above her, pale and wet with tears, was Page's beloved face.

Chapter 9

It was not so bad to be dead. Everything smelled of lavender. The blankets felt soft as fur. Annie opened her eyes. The sun had turned pink. No, the glass in the window was pink, and the sun streaming through it tinted the walls. She was in a room, a large room, and very grand. A rug in a geometric design of purple and gold occupied the middle of the floor. Fragile-looking chairs were grouped around it. In one of these chairs, pulled a little apart from the others, sat a cloaked and hooded figure.

Annie struggled into a sitting position. Her whole body ached. It more than ached—each of her limbs felt connected to her trunk by a wire that had been pulled too tight. Even her tendons ached. Even her teeth.

As soon as she sat up, the person in the chair rose and hurried for the door.

"Wait!" Annie wrestled with the bedclothes, but they proved too much for her. She sagged against the headboard, exhausted.

When she opened her eyes a second time a stern-looking

gentleman was sitting where the cloaked figure had been. The light in the room had turned from pink to gray.

"Ah," the man said, peering at Annie through little round glasses, "finally ready to face the day, are we?" He gave her a sour smile and approached the bed. She shrank away from him.

"Now, now. Doctor is your friend."

He took her wrist between his fingers and put his other hand to her forehead. His skin felt like the shed skin of a snake.

"No apparent disease. No significant injury. And yet they insist on these repeated examinations, as though I, *I*, had missed something!"

He had been speaking to the headboard, but now he looked at her irritably. "Have you sustained any puncture marks or lacerations? Are you hiding from me any wound festering, suppurating, or otherwise consequential? Well? *Well?*"

Annie shook her head. She wasn't sure she didn't have any of those things, but she was sure she wouldn't tell him if she had.

He dropped her wrist on the bed. "I'll have some food sent up shortly. In the meantime, drink this."

"What is it?"

"It's medicine, which Doctor prescribes and Patient takes."

"I thought you said I wasn't sick."

"I spoke only of the body. The mind, however"—he tapped her forehead—"what you experienced would drive most people quite mad."

"I am not mad."

"Drink! Drink, drink, drink. Or Nurse will have to come and make you drink."

⁓

When she woke a third time it was with the feeling of having slept for days. The muscle aches were gone, replaced by a strange puffy feeling, as though her skin was only just holding her insides in. Vaguely she remembered a nurse helping her negotiate a chamber pot and spooning something sweet into her mouth. She could taste it now—awful.

With a mighty effort, she got both feet onto the floor and staggered over to the window. The pink sun shone in the pink sky. Annie opened the window and stuck her head out. The air was cold. Delicious. Many stories below lay the gardens. Wildflowers grew in tidy rectangles around a fountain. She could pick out some of Gregor's favorites: jewelweed, skull-cap, bloodroot, baneberry. The lawn spread like a skirt around the palace walls. Vivid green grass showed through the snow in patches. The color of the grass reminded her of something, though she couldn't say what. At the end of the lawn a forest grew thick and dark. A pleasure forest, it must be, where lords and ladies could hunt or picnic in the safety of their own grounds. Odd. The whole garden was beautiful and odd.

A few feet beneath her window clustered the fluted leaves and delicate pink-tinged flowers of a bindweed vine. She leaned down to try to pick a flower but couldn't reach far enough.

In addition to the bed and chairs and a number of comically small tables, the room contained a wardrobe. Her clothes had been washed and ironed and hung on satin hangers. Her dress looked like a flat, headless girl. Annie felt in all the pockets. Gregor's rock and the ringstone she had stolen from Uncle Jock were still hidden in the hem. The lock of Page's hair was safe, too, somewhat curlier for having been washed and dried. But the book—the paper crumbled at her touch. The ink had run in gray streaks down the page. Even the gold had flaked off of the letters in Chilton Smalle's name. It was ridiculous to feel so sad. She hadn't been able to read it anyway. She set the book down beside her neatly folded, lavender-scented socks.

She searched the wardrobe and then the room, but the ringstone from the pit was missing, and so were the red shoes.

The room had two doors. One, which the hooded figure had passed through, was locked. The other led to a cold staircase that ended discouragingly at the lav. There was nothing to do then but wait. At last the nurse appeared carrying a bowl of some kind of custard, but as soon as she saw Annie up and about she turned around and left. The doctor arrived a few minutes later. He took her pulse.

"Hmm, somewhat thready. Too much activity today." The doctor patted the mattress. "Back to bed, young lady."

"I want to know why the door is locked."

"I'll have the nurse come up with a proper meal for you immediately. Make sure you eat everything. You are looking poorly."

"I feel good. I just want to know—"

"One does not feel good, one feels well."

"I feel well, then!"

"You do not feel well. You remain in a mentally weakened state. It has only been . . ." He caught himself.

"How long?"

"The nurse will be back soon. Eat everything."

"How long!"

But he had gone.

As promised, the nurse returned with a tray crammed with weird delicacies: chicken livers in wine reduction, rabbit fricassee with orange jelly, green beans heaped with onions curled like bows. She stayed to watch Annie eat, but Annie spent so long carving a single green bean that finally the nurse scraped her chair back with an impatient noise and went to the door.

The key she took from her pocket was made of iron. It was three inches long with rounded sides and a single tooth at the end about the length of a thumbnail. The nurse turned the key left in the keyhole, jiggled it a bit, then turned it farther left, revolving the lock. She repeated the motions on the other side of the door, locking Annie in.

Annie sighed and pushed the tray away. If only she had something to use in the lock. If only the green beans weren't so salty. She eyed her water glass. The water had a milky tinge, and when she dipped her pinky in, yes, sweet, horrible. In the end, she drank as little as she could, but it was enough.

❧

She awoke to darkness. The air in the room was frigid. *The window*, she thought. *I must have left the window unlatched.*

The curtains sighed against the casement. She felt the mattress give slightly beneath her.

"Who . . . ?"

Two neat points of pressure on her hip, now four, six, eight, climbing over her shoulder. She reached a hand out from under the covers and touched soft fur, cold from the night air. Of course they had found her. They always did.

❧

The next morning the cats were gone, but orange and brown hairs clung to the blankets. Annie hurried to the window.

The bindweed had grown since yesterday. The closest leaves lapped the windowsill. A rime of frost coated the sill and the windowpanes, but there was no frost on the leaves of the vine. Puzzled, Annie reached out to touch a leaf, then pulled her hand back quickly. The leaf was warm. Tentatively, she reached her hand out again—the petals were warm too, and the stem was almost hot. She looked down at the green circles burned into the white lawn, and snapped a flower off the vine.

Immediately, the flower wilted. She put the flower in her half-full water glass. The stem lifted. The petals deepened to a darker pink.

❧

The cats returned after dark. They went straight to her untouched dinner tray: bread pudding doused in cream and a tiny quail floating on its back in a pool of sauce, two delicate paper pom-poms where its feet should be.

Prudence buried her face in the cream. Izzy hunched over the quail carcass, cracking bones.

"Izzy, stop!"

He let her take it, but barely. Annie studied the smooth leg bone, the prominence at one end where it fit into the hip socket, split and sharpened now by Izzy's chewing.

It shouldn't have worked. It didn't work, the first fifty tries. And then, with the cats watching her lazily from the bed, and her palms sweating, and the greasy bone-key slipping, it did.

Annie opened the door, just a crack, and peered out into the hall. It was empty.

Her old clothes felt good, scratchy and stiff after the fine fabric of the nightgown, but hers. The hall stretched immensely long in both directions, punctuated by candles in wall sconces and carpeted in purple, green, and gold. There were doors on either side, all closed. At one end she could see a long, thin window, like an arrow slit, and below it the first few steps of a staircase.

Down, down, down the stairs she went, past a great black and white tiled hall, past a pink and gold ballroom, past a green and burgundy billiards room, past the steamy kitchen where the scullery boys were washing dishes. Finally the steps ended at a plain wooden door. She opened it.

A crushed stone path led around the wall of the palace to the gardens. Lanterns of colored glass lit the path and she watched her hands turn blue, then red, then purple as she stepped through pools of light. Bits of gravel poked her feet through her socks.

She passed banks of flowers and neatly groomed raspberry bushes laden with berries. To her right a wild rose had been trained to a fragile network of lattice. The lawn, clear of snow now and such a vivid a green it was almost sickening, spread out before her. The colors in the garden seemed sinister to her now, not beautiful. She felt sorry for the plants.

❧

Stepping among the trees of the pleasure forest, Annie felt a queer thrill, part fear, part joy. She was in danger; she was safe. She was lost; she was on the path. She wondered if the lords and ladies had the same feeling when they entered the pleasure forest, if that was the point.

Annie followed the path until it emerged on the other side of the forest, crossing several more yards of lawn before joining a path that ran along the base of a high stone wall. She had reached the border of the palace grounds. Statues lined the path at precise intervals: a stone Cupid aimed his arrow at a stone fawn. A stone goose curved its neck over stone eggs. The whole place had a forgotten, melancholy air, as though the statues were waiting for someone to arrive who never did.

Annie turned left at the wall, but the path soon disappeared beneath the tangles of an errant bracka hedge. She smiled a little at that. Bracka bushes would always have their way, royal gardeners or no.

Picking her way around the hedge, she was struck by the quiet of the pleasure forest. Even the smells seemed muted, without the spice and rot she remembered from the forest of

Dour County. She ran a finger over the bark of the nearest tree. It felt real enough. Yet those boulders just ahead: there was something too orderly about them. They reminded her of the rocks she had climbed to reach the castle gates. And they felt... they were hollow! Annie knocked against the rock again, enjoying the sound.

"Who is there?"

The voice struck Annie like an arrow. She dropped to her knees.

"Hello? Is someone there?"

That voice. *Oh, that voice.*

She started to crawl, fast, around the base of the rocks. Pine needles pricked her hands. She could hear herself panting.

"Please! You are frightening me. Tell me who is there!"

It's me! It's me! But the words caught in her throat. She burst around the edge of the rock pile, then reared back in panic. Inches from her face hung the massive head and heavy, narrow jaws of a kinderstalk. One side of its muzzle rose in a snarl. The tongue was very red. The fangs were long, white at the tips, yellow where they met the gums. But most frightening of all were the eyes, round and blank, filmed over with milky white. The kinderstalk was blind. Did she have a chance, then? Annie inched backward. The animal snarled and advanced. One great paw, bigger than a man's foot, pinned her right hand to the ground.

She could hear someone whimpering and thought, *That must be me.* Then she heard a strange low sound, almost like barking. The kinderstalk's ears pricked up. A hooded figure emerged from the shelter of the rocks, holding a torch. The kinderstalk trotted over and sat down beside the figure, docile as a dog. The figure laid a slender hand on the kinderstalk's head—a woman's hand.

At the sight of the hand, Annie began to tremble. The figure set the torch in the earth and raised both hands to her hood. Long pale hair, nearly white, hung around her shoulders. She held out her arms.

Chapter 10

Annie buried her face in Page's hair, breathing in the familiar scent of ink and old leather. She drew back from her sister just far enough to peer into her face. Tears leaked from the corners of Page's eyes and her nose was running, but she looked happy.

"Come inside," Page said, mopping at her face with a sleeve.

Annie let go of her reluctantly. Page picked up a cane leaning against the side of the rock shelter. She walked with a fluid, firm step, the cane moving like a part of her body. Annie felt happy and a little lost to see that her sister no longer needed crutches.

The kinderstalk followed them in. Annie edged away from it, but Page smiled. "He won't hurt you."

It was more a cave than a house, with only a jagged space between two boulders to serve as an entrance. Torches illuminated the walls and low ceiling, all formed of the same rocks that were not rocks. A straw pallet and a three-legged stool made up the furniture. From a hook close to the entrance hung a clutch of dead rabbits.

"Can I come stay here with you?"

It took Page a moment to answer.

"I have a room at the palace. I only stay here sometimes, to keep Sharta company."

"The kinderstalk?" Annie gaped. "You named it?"

"Him. And he already had a name."

Annie's heart felt like it was being squeezed tight in someone's fist. "I saw you, the night the kinderstalk chased me. And you saw me."

"Yes."

"It wasn't a dream."

"No."

"You knew I was here. You knew I was locked in that room."

"Yes." Page's voice was soft, urgent. "But, Annie, ask yourself what—who—could possibly keep me away from you?"

Annie studied the empty face of one of the dead rabbits.

"Was it the king?"

Page nodded. "I'm not free here either, not really." She gestured around the cave. "Sharta has his little prison, and I have mine."

"But why are you here? I don't understand."

Page studied her for a long moment. At last she spoke.

"You didn't get my letters."

"You wrote me letters? Uncle Jock must have . . . they told me you were dead!" Annie wailed.

"Shh, sweetheart. I'm not dead."

"F-f-fever, he said. He burned your books!"

"He's a villain."

"How many letters?"

"Every week. Sometimes every day."

Annie wiped her nose with her sleeve.

"I wish the kinderstalk would kill him."

Page smiled. "I should tell you not to say such things." She handed Annie a handkerchief. The fabric was very soft. A triangle of letters was embroidered in one corner, *P-U-T*, with the *U* at the top and bigger than the other letters. Annie pointed to it.

"What does that mean?"

Page blushed. "Oh, that's nothing. Everything has to be so fancy here. You'd better blow your nose."

"Why are you a prisoner like me?" Annie asked.

"Well, we both arrived here the same way. I came with Sharta. You came with many, many more of his kind."

"I didn't come *with* the kinderstalk! I was running away from them!"

"I think the king believes that now. He took some convincing. You're lucky I found your slipper."

"My slipper?" Annie felt the conversation wheeling away from her. She had the ugly feeling of being the butt of a joke, but there was only Page, watching her anxiously, and the kinderstalk. It lay at her sister's feet, eyes closed, ears erect.

Page reached into the pocket of her cloak. "We only opened the door far enough to pull you inside, but the kinderstalk scattered. They left this."

It was the right shoe, the one with Prue's face on it. Something had punctured the sole in several places.

"I showed this slipper to the king." Page shook the shoe in the air. "I told him, 'She barely escaped with her life! She warned us to close the doors! And now you want to throw her in the dungeon?'"

Annie touched one of the holes in the leather. Definitely a tooth. "I was in the dungeon?"

"For twelve minutes. He agreed to let you out, on three conditions."

"If I took my medicine?"

"Yes. And I was not allowed to visit you."

"That medicine, it's the same potion they give the plants to make them bloom."

"It's harmless, that stuff. It might even be salutary."

Before, when she used a word like that, Page would have grinned, and waited, and Annie would have asked what it meant. They would have made a game of it.

Instead Annie asked, "What was the third condition?"

Page had been leaning close to Annie, her face eager. Now she sat up straight and stiff. A pink spot appeared on each cheek.

"We should go now. It will be light soon, and it's better if they don't know you left the room."

Annie didn't budge. "You said you came here with the kinderstalk? How? What happened? Why did you leave?"

Page studied her hands. There was a smudge of ink on the right ring finger. "All this time, when I imagined you reading my letters, it felt like you were here with me. I shared everything with you. And now you're here, you're really here, and you don't know any of it, and we feel so far apart."

Annie didn't know what to say.

Page took the kinderstalk's long jaws in her hands. She murmured something that made its ears stiffen, then relax. Slowly, the big head swung toward Annie. The snout lifted, searching the air. Without knowing quite what she was doing, Annie extended her hand. Cold nose, hot chuff of breath, a prickle of whiskers in her palm.

Page took her arm. "Come on."

Page stopped just long enough to grab the torch, then plunged through the trees, beating bracka bushes aside with her cane. Annie followed her at a trot.

"Page, wait. Page, slow down." A branch bounced off her sister's cane and snapped against her thigh.

"Page! *Stop*."

Page turned. Her face looked fierce in the torchlight.

"Give me the torch," Annie said.

"What? Why? You don't know where you're going."

Annie hesitated, just for a second. "I can't see. You're walking too fast."

Page pinched her lips together. "Fine. But stay close behind me."

Any tree would do. The snow that had burned away so quickly from the lawn still clung to their shaded roots. Still, she waited until they had nearly reached the edge of the pleasure forest. Then she slowed, pretended to stumble, and plunged the torch into a patch of snow and sodden leaves.

Darkness dropped over them like a shroud. Page screamed. For a moment, in the shame that rushed over her as fast as the dark, Annie wondered if her dark sight had deserted her. Then objects began to pick themselves out of the blackness— the bulky contours of a tree trunk, the spreading fineness of branches, an emerging bud.

"Annie! Where are you?"

"I'm right here." Annie touched her sister's hand. Page jumped.

"I can feel you, but I don't . . . I can't . . . oh, I *hate* it!" Page's voice was nearly a wail.

"I have matches. Wait, it's almost lit." Annie counted to twenty, then made the sounds of fumbling. She was glad her sister could not see her face.

The torch hissed into light. Page lunged for it like a drowning person. So this question, at least, was answered. Page could speak to the kinderstalk, but only Annie could see in the dark.

From the top of the stairs Page walked straight to Annie's door. Of course she would know where the room was, but still, it hurt to see her act as though she had been to visit Annie a hundred times before.

"I *did* visit you. I snuck in when you were asleep. I even read to you a few times about abnormal topography." She forced a smile and lifted her hand to tuck a piece of hair behind Annie's ear. "You're as tall as I am."

"Page, I have something important to tell the king. It's why I came."

Her sister's eyes were light blue, very clear, like water from a spring. Now she did touch Annie's face, briefly. Annie turned her cheek into her palm. She would forgive her anything. Everything.

"I'll be back for you tomorrow morning," Page said. "We'll talk more then. Sleep well. And don't . . . don't worry."

Annie woke to find Page sitting next to her in bed, reading. Her hair had been looped and braided into an elaborate crown. On top of her real hair was a tower of what looked like someone else's hair, all of it held together by jeweled combs. She wore a red velvet dress embroidered at the bust and hem with gold curlicues. Her lips were painted red to match her dress. Strangest of all, her face was dusted with white powder and her eyebrows had been shaped into high, surprised-looking arches. Annie felt a little afraid of her, until she noticed the brown and white cat hairs clinging to the lap of her dress. Prudence sat at the end of the bed washing her face.

"Sleepyhead. I was just about to wake you."

Annie scooted up from under the covers and leaned over her sister's shoulder to see what she was reading. Page showed her the cover. *Topographical Anomalies of the Frigian Glacier.*

"Dull?"

"Extremely."

"Page, I found your book! I took it from Aunt Prim. It had

your notes in it but the rest was written in some language I couldn't read. It isn't even a book, really, just a paper hidden inside another book."

Page had gone pale. "May I see it?"

Annie jumped up and ran to the wardrobe. "It was in my pocket when they washed my dress. The ink washed away."

Page held the book for a moment without opening it. Quickly, she lifted the cover, looked at the watery streaks that had once been letters, and closed it again. Her fingers reached for the locket she had worn since childhood, a gift from their parents. It looked plain and dull against the elaborate dress.

"You said Aunt Prim had this? Not Uncle Jock?"

"Aunt Prim. I don't think he knew she had it."

"That's good."

"Why? What did it say?"

"I never figured it out, but I think its a message from Mother and Father. I was trying to translate it when—" She broke off. "You'd better get dressed. We're going to have breakfast with the king."

Annie looked at a puddle of brown fabric on the floor by her feet. She hadn't bothered to hang up her dress last night, and now it was not only stained, threadbare, and two sizes too small, but wrinkled.

"Not in that. In this."

Page reached past her into the wardrobe and took out a green dress. Not a dress, a gown. A woman's gown. The waist nipped in, the skirt flounced out. The sleeves were embroidered with a pattern of silver vines.

"I'm sure you'll hate it, but it was the least lacey one I could find."

"I don't hate it."

"Oh. Well, good."

"Page?"

"There are slippers as well. They have a bit of a heel. You're too young for that, but—"

"Why did you leave? How did you get here?"

Page had been holding the green dress up to her body. Now she lowered her arms, as though the dress had become too heavy for her. It pooled around her feet.

"Oh, Annie." She walked over and sat down on the bed. Annie watched a cat hair on the collar of her dress flutter each time she breathed. "It's a horrible story. The first part, anyway."

"Tell me!"

"Uncle Jock sold me to the Drop." She touched the handle of her cane. "He couldn't have gotten much for me."

Annie moved to put her arms around her sister, but Page leaned away. "Let me get it over with. He'd sent you and Aunt Prim to market, remember? A man came to the house. I'd never seen anyone so ugly. Gray skin like milk gone bad, and beady eyes."

"Did he have a scar, like this?" Annie traced a line down the middle of her scalp.

Page shook her head. "No scar, but—" Her eyes widened. "A wound. He was wounded there. How did you know? Oh, Annie, tell me Uncle Jock didn't—"

"He did. He tried. I'll tell you, but finish the story."

"Uncle Jock and this ugly man, they tied me up in a wagon with the rain cover on it. I was trying to translate the paper when they grabbed me. Aunt Prim must have picked it up." She shook her head. "I knew where they were taking me. Uncle Jock forced me to drink something awful, so I wouldn't fight." She gripped both Annie's hands tightly in her own. "Sharta attacked the wagon, Sharta and his mate. They saved me."

"Kinderstalk saved you?" Annie blurted. "But why? Why not kill you?"

"Annie, shh, just listen. Uncle Jock ran at the first sight of Sharta, of course. But the other man fought. I couldn't see because of the wagon cover, but I could hear—oh, it was awful! Sharta fought the man and his mate freed me. When she jumped into the wagon bed . . . you can imagine what I thought. But she chewed through the ropes. She pulled me by the back of my dress, here." Page touched the nape of her neck. "I saw the ugly man lying on the ground, bleeding from his head. I thought Sharta had killed him. And Sharta—"

"He made Sharta blind?"

"Yes. I don't remember much after that. Whatever they'd given me to drink made me sleep. I woke a few times and it felt as if I were flying, but I think—I think Sharta's mate carried me on her back. The next thing I knew I was tied up again, this time by the king's guards. I learned later that they found us together, Sharta and I, outside the same gates where we found you. They put him in a cage and let all the lords and ladies in to look. The 'Blind Beast' they called him."

"And now you can speak to him?"

"His language is Hippa." The word sounded like a cough.

"Hippa?" Annie coughed back.

"That was good!" Page smiled. "You would hardly believe how difficult it was to learn. The difference between one sound and another can be so small, but the *meaning* . . . I still make mistakes all the time. But yes, we talk together. He and his mate had a message of their own for the king."

"What is it?

"Not now, Miss Curious." She picked the green gown up off the floor. "Will you put this on and wash your face, and come meet the king?"

Annie walked to the window. Through the glass she could see the tips of the trees in the pleasure forest, waving like kelp in a pink sea. She thought of Gregor, who loved the sea.

"Should I braid my hair?'

"Leave it loose. It's so pretty loose."

Twenty minutes later, Annie descended the stairs for a second time to meet Page in the black and white tiled hall. She kept forgetting she didn't have to sneak, and snuck. Not that it was easy to move unnoticed in this dress. It rustled. It pinched. It caught itself on everything. And the shoes: wobble, wobble, wobble down the stairs.

Page looked as small as a toy at the far end of hall. She led Annie along an arched corridor. The curved ceiling was painted gold. The walls were lined with portraits. On one side a row of dimpled ladies reclined against cushions; on the other a line of dark-haired men posed beside the bodies of dead kinder-stalk.

Gilt-edged mirrors reaching to the floor hung between the portraits on Annie's left, reflecting the sunlight that filtered through the colored windowpanes and washing the painted ladies in shades of mauve and indigo.

Page stopped in front of one of the mirrors and tapped on the glass. Instantly the mirror swung open like a door and revealed a small, warmly lit chamber. The king was sitting in an armchair by the window. He looked up when they entered.

The king was so handsome that Annie found it embarrassing to look at him. He had glossy black hair that waved over his forehead and a red mouth that pouted like a woman's. But his hands, lightly gripping the arms of his chair, were as big as a laborer's. Annie decided immediately that he was vain. She glanced at the mirror over the fireplace and met his eyes there. He had been studying her, studying him.

The king gestured to two chairs facing his own. Through the window, Annie could see the courtyard and the massive doors that had been shut against her the night she arrived. They were shut now.

A servant emerged through the mirrored door carrying a tray of tea and chocolate. Pastries fanned across a plate, each shaped like a different kind of leaf: oak, maple, bay. The king picked up a bay leaf and bit into it. Flakes of dough fell onto his lap, staining the gray silk with spots of oil. The servant used a little silver brush to sweep the crumbs into a napkin.

Annie ate five pastries. The first bite dissolved in her mouth in a rush of sugar and butter; after that, she hardly noticed the taste. She forgot to thank the servant when he poured her a second cup of chocolate. She set down her cup and found Page and the king both looking at her, the king with bemusement, Page with mortification and a hint of alarm.

"I trust you have found your accommodations satisfactory, Miss Trewitt?" the king said.

"Yes, Your Highness." If he had not been so handsome, and not been the king, she might have told him he would be starving too if he'd had the doctor in charge of his meals.

"I am pleased to hear it." He flicked his fingers at the servant, who disappeared through the mirrored door.

The king settled back in his chair and smiled broadly at Annie. "Your sister has not been very forthcoming about your reasons for visiting the palace, Miss Trewitt. May I indulge myself a moment in letting you know what I imagine?"

Annie nodded, realizing as she did so that he had not asked the kind of question that waited for an answer.

"I imagine you are here to do me great harm, Miss Trewitt. I imagine you have an army of kinderstalk waiting to rescue your sister from a most wicked king. Is that not what she has written you, in her many dozens of letters? Were they not all accounts of my great wickedness?" His hands had become clenched on the arms of the chair. He folded them in his lap and smiled more broadly than ever. "I imagine, Miss Trewitt, that at this very moment, you have merely to snap your fingers and summon that army of kinderstalk to your side. Am I wrong to imagine such things, when in all the history of Howland, so far as any of my scholars can tell me, no person has survived an encounter with the kinderstalk such as yours, save, perhaps, your dear sister?"

Annie sat dumb as a stump. His words seemed like a net thrown over her and cinched tight, so anything she might have thought to say could not reach her lips.

"Have I imagined wrongly, Miss Trewitt?" said the king. "Do tell me so."

"Your Highness," Page said in a low voice. "Remember you are speaking to a child."

The king looked from Page to Annie. For a long time he said nothing. Then he appeared to make a decision. He took off his crown and set it on the table next to his chair. His hair, so dense and shiny black that it appeared to have been lacquered, held the crown's imprint. Annie wondered if it looked like that even when he slept.

When he smiled again there was something like warmth in it.

"A jest, rather poorly executed." He dipped his head in a bow. "Forgive me."

Again Annie nodded, though she had no clear sense of what she had agreed to, or what was forgiven.

"Lady Trewitt requested this interview on your behalf, Miss Trewitt. What is it you wish to tell me?"

"Lady Trewitt?" asked Annie.

The king inclined his head toward Page. "She hasn't shared our news with you yet?"

Annie turned to her sister. "Page?"

"I thought at a later time," Page murmured.

"Very well. Such news is best savored, perhaps. Now, Miss Trewitt, your information?"

But Annie's mouth had gone dry. She looked at Page's hands twisted together in her lap.

"Go on, Annie," Page said quietly.

So she told them about the Drop, and the orphanage, and the children working at night. She told them what a runout was and what they did to them. She told them about seeing Gibbet in the wood, and the kinderstalk on its hind legs, and the rabbits; she told them about the pit with its hidden treasure and the tunnel to the river. She did not tell them that she could see in the dark, and, for some reason she didn't understand, she did not tell them about Beatrice and Serena.

For a long time, the only sounds in the room were Annie's voice and the occasional pop and hiss of logs in the fire. The king listened with his eyes half-closed, his steepled fingers pressed to his lips. Page stared intently at the fire, as though it were telling the story.

When she had finished speaking, the king surprised her by fixing her another cup of chocolate. The chocolate itself was scalding hot and very bitter; he added cream and three spoonfuls of sugar, then mixed it all together carefully. It tasted divine.

The king leaned back, steepling his fingers again as he regarded her. All of his postures, even the most casual, seemed studied.

"The ringstone that was recovered from among your

possessions was of exceptional quality. You believe it to have been mined at the Drop?"

"As I told you, the children mine the white stone. They can get into the narrow spaces between the rocks." Page shot her a look. "Your Highness," Annie added.

The king smiled coldly. "Pardon me for wishing to clarify some of the more important points in this narrative."

"Of course, Your Highness."

"When you observed Mr. Gibbet with the kinderstalk, are you certain they were speaking?"

"Yes."

"And you believe Mr. Gibbet and his men are smuggling ringstone out of the country by way of the West River?"

"I do."

The king turned to Page. "The foreign currency she found—that is Frigia's coin, and Brineland's, and Redonda's."

"It is just as Sharta warned us," Page said. "Gibbet is planning—"

"Quiet!" The king gestured toward Annie. "That is the business of the crown, and none of hers."

"For heaven's sake, Terr! She's my sister!" Annie and the king both looked at Page, startled.

Terr?

Page blushed. "Your Highness, she risked her life to come here and tell you what she knows. Her information corroborates what Sharta has told us. I see no reason not to be open."

The king ignored her.

"Miss Trewitt, how is it that you knew the kinderstalk would attack the palace when they did?"

"I didn't know."

"Your Highness, *she* was the target—" Page started to interrupt, but the king wagged a finger in the air and she fell silent. Annie struggled against a sudden wave of hatred for him.

"I'd arrived in Magnifica that day and had just learned about the engagement party," Annie said. "I thought it would be my best chance to, well, to enter the grounds unnoticed, so I took it." She trailed off, uncertain. Nobody spoke. "I could not think of another way to reach you, Your Highness, and Gregor . . . all the children at the Drop, it is bad for them there."

When another minute passed without anyone saying anything, Annie stood up and walked over to the window. She didn't know if that was something you were allowed to do without permission from the king. She hoped it wasn't.

Outside, blooming dogwood trees grew along the perimeter of the courtyard, their black branches lacy with frost. The sun was shining and the paving stones had been swept clear of snow, and around the base of each tree white petals mixed with the white snow.

Behind her, the king and Page had begun a whispered conversation, their heads bent together. A lock of Page's hair touched the king's shoulder. Suddenly the king jerked upright and slammed his fist on the table so hard that the cups jumped in their saucers.

"I thought only *you* could speak to the beasts!" he roared at Page. "This changes everything!"

"How could I have known? I don't know where he learned! If you had let me speak to her when she first arrived, perhaps

Gibbet's plans would not have advanced so far!" Page paused, breathing hard. Both of them seemed to have forgotten Annie was in the room.

"It isn't too late to stop Gibbet," Page went on. "You have Sharta. You have me. Let's try. Let's talk to them." Page's voice sounded low and tense, and something else, something Annie didn't recognize from her sister. She was pleading with him.

Annie's heart hammered high in her chest, as though it would burst from between her collarbones.

"The beast is useless," the king hissed. "*You* are useless!" He gestured contemptuously at Annie. "She cannot speak to them, can she? So how is it she knows so much? So much more than you? Have you been keeping secrets from me?"

Page shook her head. Tears cut tracks through the white powder on her face. "You are cruel."

"Well?" the king persisted. "Well?" He leaned forward across the table, his face inches from hers. Page shrank back until it seemed the chair would swallow her.

"What's the matter, kinderstalk got your tongue?" he sneered.

"I will *never* marry you!" Page spat out. The king blanched, then raised his arm over his head, hand balled into a fist. What happened next was so strange that Annie could not be sure afterward what was real and what she had imagined.

Page cried out, but the sound was immediately swallowed by another sound—snarling. In an instant Annie was between the king and Page, her body rigid as a shield. The king tried to push

her aside, and then she was at his throat. The weight of her body striking his chest knocked the king backward. The edge of his throne caught him behind the knees, and the throne, several hundred pounds of oak, brocade, and ringstone, screeched across the tile floor and slammed into the bookcase behind it.

Annie came to her senses with her hands around the king's neck. She scrambled off his lap and backed away, eyeing him warily. Her palms felt damp, but when she moved to dry them on her dress she saw that they were wet with blood, not sweat. The blood was coming from the tips of her fingers.

Three red gashes ran from the corner of the king's right eye down his cheek and over his jaw. Blood dripped onto his gray silk vest. The king looked down at himself and when he raised his eyes, Annie could see that he was frightened. Annie was too—she knew she should go for help, but somehow all she could do was rub her hands, over and over, against the front of her dress.

Page stepped out of her petticoat and folded it into a square. She pressed the cloth against the wounds. Her fingers drifted through the damp hair stuck to the king's forehead. His eyes closed.

"Annie, you must find the doctor. If anyone asks you, tell them the king has retired for the day."

Annie nodded dumbly and turned to go.

"Wait." With her free hand, Page smoothed Annie's hair down behind her ears, rubbed a fleck of blood from her cheek. "Wipe your hands on my dress. It won't show on the red. Good. Now try to smile, and remember to curtsy if you pass anyone of rank. And, Annie, don't tell anyone, not even the doctor, that you—don't explain."

Once more, Annie turned to go. This time it was the king's voice that stopped her.

"I would never have hurt her."

Annie left the room.

Chapter 11

The bindweed outside her window had crept over the sill and wrapped itself around the window frame. Cone-shaped flowers, white with purple veins, crowded against the glass. Two weeks had passed since she attacked the king.

"He's fine," Page told her. "Maybe a bit subdued."

"Will you marry him?" Annie asked.

Page sighed. "I don't know. I said I would. That was the third condition, to get you out of the dungeon."

"Do you . . . are you in love with him?"

"No. Sometimes. He's not always so—"

Arrogant? Bloodthirsty? Evil?

"—imperious. And what he said, at the end. It's true. He would never hurt me."

"He was going to hit you!"

Page met Annie's eyes. "He wasn't. He was reaching for the bell pull. To call the servant."

Annie took a moment to digest this and found she couldn't.

"I know you didn't mean to hurt him. You were only try-ing to protect me." She looked down at her gloved hands. "I have never seen you like that before."

That wasn't me! Annie wanted to cry, but she couldn't. Whatever part of her had attacked the king was as real as the part that knew how to wait quietly, to ask before taking.

She laced her bare fingers through her sister's satin-covered ones. "I'm sorry."

Page looked up, her eyes bright. "I do love him. I love him and half the time I don't even like him." She smiled, surprised, it seemed, to hear herself say the words. "In a way, I think he respects you because of this. Everyone here has to act as if he's the smartest, wittiest, most marvelous person they've ever met, so he never knows when he's being a bore. I'm not sure he even knows when he's being cruel. He admires people who are honest. And you, little one, can't help but be honest."

Not always, Annie thought. *You don't know everything.*

Page gave her hand a squeeze and unlaced their fingers. "He's furious, of course. His looks are practically ruined."

Annie decided it was time to change the subject.

"Will the king put Gibbet in the dungeon for smuggling?"

"I think it's gone beyond that, Annie."

"He won't let him get away with it!"

"Of course not." She paused. "Have you considered what Gibbet's buying in exchange for all that stone?"

Annie thought back to the cove at Witch's Hand, the empty coffin-shaped boxes stacked by the boats.

"Muskets."

"Not only those. Remember the foreign coins you found? Kings take an interest in what happens in their neighboring countries. I think Gibbet is paying them *not* to be interested. I think he's planning to seize the crown. And when he does, they'll let him."

❧

Page wanted to know everything that had happened to Annie since she left Uncle Jock's. Annie wanted to know when the king would rescue Gregor from the Drop.

"When?" Annie asked for the hundredth time that morning. Page leaned down to inspect a mat in Sharta's fur. Her hair swung forward to hide her face.

"Soon. He's meeting with his advisors every day." She tugged at the mat with her own gold comb.

"What does he need advisors for? Doesn't he have an army? Couldn't he just send an army?"

Page rested her forehead on the kinderstalk's back. She closed her eyes. "Annie, from what you've told me . . . have you considered that Gregor may not be alive?"

"Of course! I don't know!" Annie shouted, and then, stubbornly, "When will the king send someone to the Drop?"

"I don't know. Soon."

"You do know! He doesn't care!"

"He does care."

"Then when?"

And round and round they went, Page alternately embarrassed, weary, awkward, and at last, angry.

"You're such a pest! Stop badgering me!"

Hurt, Annie turned away. "You've taken his side."

"This isn't you and me against Uncle Jock anymore," Page snapped, and strode out of the shelter.

Annie stared after her until a pressure against her hip made her look down. The kinderstalk stood beside her. Carefully, she let one hand rest on his head.

~

An army of women burst into Annie's room the next morning. They bore brushes, curlers, pots and jars, swaths of silk and lace, a pincushion the size of a hedgehog.

"What is all this?" Annie asked, edging away.

"Why, for the reception, Miss! Measurements first, then hair and face, then the dress should be just ready."

There commenced such a poking, pushing, and prodding that Annie took a silent vow: if Page married the king, and if Annie was to live here as some kind of princess, she would stay with Sharta and wear her own old dress every day. Or perhaps, she amended, as a maid dropped a petticoat of softest linen over her head, perhaps she would allow them to make her some underwear.

Annie had encountered various lords and ladies during her walks around the palace with Page, a blur of wigs and lace and pursed lips and cold eyes. The maids were different. If they noticed her awkwardness they gave no sign of it, except perhaps through little flurries of praise.

"What a lovely color against Miss's complexion!"

"Straight as a statue Miss stands!"

"Such pretty hair Miss has!"

One of the maids, Pamela, decided that because Annie had such a great quantity of her own hair, and the color was so very dark, and the darkest wig on hand not quite dark enough, that they would make do with what they called a "natural" style.

"Only, Miss . . ." Pamela sounded nervous.

"What is it?" Annie asked.

"The patch of white here, at the nape. Would you like it to show, or not to show? Or should I powder the whole? Or perhaps a coil at the back, and the rest on top?"

Annie touched the back of her head, but the white hair didn't feel any different from the rest. Suddenly, like a blow to the stomach, she missed Gregor. He would have found the white patch interesting, an oddity of nature, neither disgusting nor beautiful, but good, because strange.

"Miss?"

"Hide it, I suppose. Whatever you like."

At last, giggling and smiling, a girl took each of Annie's hands and led her to the mirror. She looked both better and worse than she had feared. Worse, because she looked like a dressed-up child, fooling herself into thinking she was a woman. Better, because the weight of her hair and the cold press of jewels at her neck made her hold her head straight and still. She looked haughty as a queen. The thought made

her blush, but the blush didn't show beneath all the powder on her face.

After the maids left, Annie spent a few minutes standing in the middle of the room, afraid to sit down on the piles of crinoline. When a knock sounded at the door she yanked it open.

"Page, you can't imagine how long . . ."

The doctor raised his eyebrows above his round glasses.

"Ah, yes. The tribulations of beauty." He looked her over. "Beauty, or its pretense."

Annie had withdrawn at the sight of him, but now he took a step toward her. "Young lady, I am to escort you to the throne room."

"Where is my sister?"

"Perhaps she is otherwise occupied? His Highness asked me to escort you."

Reluctantly, Annie extended her hand. Instead of tucking it under his arm as she had seen the lords and ladies do around the palace, the doctor lifted her hand to his face. For a horrible moment she thought he would kiss it, but instead he pushed his glasses onto his forehead and peered at her fingers. Her nails seemed to interest him most.

"Of average length and sharpness, I should say," he murmured.

Annie pulled her hand away. The maids had left a pair of satin elbow-length gloves that she had judged too ridiculous to wear, but now she put them on gratefully.

The doctor led her downstairs and across the great open

chamber of black and white tiles. They walked through the same corridor that Annie had visited with Page, the ladies in the portraits reclining against the same cushions, the lords leering down at the same slain kinderstalk. Annie's image flashed in the mirrors that hung between each portrait: herself, a stranger, herself, a stranger.

They reached the end of the corridor and stopped before a pair of carved double doors. The doctor paused, his hands on the door handles. He cocked an eyebrow at Annie.

"Ready?"

"Why am I here? What is this about?"

The doctor smiled his sour smile. "I believe you are to be presented with an award of some kind."

An award?

The doctor pushed open the doors.

"Miss Annie Trewitt," he announced, and bowed low. He moved aside and held out his hand. Annie stepped forward, taking his cold fingers in her colder ones. She was glad the doctor had announced her, for she could barely remember her own name, let alone speak it. Every inch of the vast room glittered with ringstone. Stones studded the high vaulted ceiling, winked out from window frames and sparkled from the inlaid floor. The king's throne, mounted on a dais, pulsed with pinkish green light, brightening the figure of the king so much that it was painful to look at him. Annie shielded her eyes, then, fearing she had been rude, dropped her hand and just stood there, squinting. The king gestured languidly with one hand and immediately filmy curtains were drawn across the windows, dimming the room enough that Annie could see properly.

She almost wished she couldn't. The room was filled, *crammed*, with lords and ladies of the court. In addition to the men at arms in their red and gold uniforms were ladies and gentlemen in waiting, cousins, aunts, uncles, distant relations, relations of the distant relations, all looking at her.

Annie curtsied as Page had taught her, then waited. When the king did nothing, she curtsied again. A ripple of laughter passed through the assembly.

"Approach."

At the sound of the king's voice the room fell silent. Annie took a step forward. The polished floor was slick as ice. By the time she reached the edge of the dais her whole body prickled with sweat.

"You may mount the dais."

A few gasps from the crowd told her this was not a usual privilege. The platform was high enough that she wished she could put her hands on the edge to steady herself, but somehow that seemed the wrong thing to do. In her nervousness she misjudged her strength. The momentum of her step carried her over the edge of the dais across the few feet still separating her from the throne. She caught herself before she ended up in the king's lap, but not before she saw a shadow of fear cross his face.

The crowd had caught its breath when Annie stumbled and still seemed to be holding it. The silence went on and on, but because the king didn't seem to care, Annie found she didn't either. Let the lords and ladies squirm for a bit. As if he had read her mind, one side of the king's mouth lifted. He was *enjoying* this. Suddenly Annie felt sad for him, though she couldn't have said exactly why.

She certainly saw why he made people stand so far away. Up close, the signs of the attack—her attack—were more obvious. The cuts on his face had been stitched and covered in plaster, the plaster then covered over with heavy powder. His skin was pale beneath what could only have been rouge on his cheeks and lips, and beneath his chin Annie could see the purple smudge of a bruise.

To Miss Annie Trewitt,
Daughter of Shar and Helen Trewitt,
Who, in the Commitment of an Action both
Selfless and Courageous,
Resulting in the Aversion of an Event of Great Violence
Intended to Our Person and Our Court,
Namely, the Attack by Beastly Hordes,
Namely, the Kinderstalk,
Has Won our Enduring Gratitude and Trust,
We Award
The Royal Medal of Honorable Distinction.

All through the ceremony, through the blaring of the trumpets, the unfurling of the scroll, the recitation of the deed, the presentation of the medal, and the bestowing of the blessing, Annie stared at that bruise. The king, in turn, never once took his eyes from her face. This, then, was how he had decided to punish her: to hold her up before the entire court as a model of bravery when only the two of them—and Page, oh, where was Page?—knew that she was little better than an animal.

At last it was over. The lords and ladies filed out, and all the light and color seemed to drain out of the room with them. Only the king, Annie, and the doctor remained. Annie was wondering how to take her leave—should she ask for permission or simply begin backing away?—when a painting on the wall opposite the windows caught her attention. The painting was a formal portrait of a group of men, each almost life size. The man in the center stood with his foot propped up on something, looking directly out from the canvas. The others looked at him. They were all finely dressed, but scattered around them were picks and shovels and scrolls of paper. Mining equipment. It must be a scene from the story Beatrice had told her, the first Terrance Uncton standing with his foot on the column of ringstone. He looked handsome and young, and a little bored with having his portrait painted. Annie's eyes slid to the figure next to him. This man was kneeling, his face at a slight angle. In one hand he held a set of scales, in the other, a whip. He wore the same elaborately curled beard and heavy sideburns as the other men, but his mouth showed plainly, a red line drawn nearly ear to ear. Something bulged against the closed lips.

To the left of the portrait hung a round ringstone plaque about the size of a dinner plate. The plaque bore an inscription, the letters rough and uneven: "Prop. of Tr. Uncton."

The double doors burst open and Page flew into the room.

When her feet slid out from under her on the slick floor, she threw out the cane, righted herself, and kept going as if nothing had happened.

She climbed the dais without a moment's hesitation—there were stairs, it turned out, that Annie hadn't seen—and reached toward the king as though she was going to grasp his sleeve. She caught herself before she touched him.

"The assayer from the Drop is here."

The king nodded to the doctor. "Quince, you may go."

The assayer was shown in, self-conscious in his riding clothes and clearly exhausted. The king's face darkened as he listened to the report. Page looked anxious. Annie felt angry. Nothing the man said differed from what she had already told them. The Drop was chipping out at twice the expected rate. *Well, of course it was. They were mining it day and night.* The stone produced at the Drop was of inferior quality than projected. *Well, yes, because all of the good stone was going into the pit at Chopper's farm.* The miners had the appearance of malnourishment. Their living conditions were substandard. *Yes, and yes.*

And were children being forced to work the mine?

"Your Highness, this I cannot verify. I noted a building fitting the description of the orphanage, but when I requested entry the individual on duty"—he pulled a much-creased paper from his pocket and consulted it—"one Silas Smirch, claimed the building was dangerously unsound, and he could not allow me to risk injury by entering. I asked to see his superior, a man named"—he consulted his paper again—"Mr. Lindsey Chopswart."

Annie pressed her hand over her mouth to keep from smiling at this completely inappropriate time. Chopper's given name was *Lindsey*?

"Mr. Chopswart was very polite in his insistence on the danger of entering the building," the assayer went on. "Or rather, his words were polite. However, his tone—I can only describe his tone as full of threat."

"Threat!" the king said.

"No actual threats were issued, Your Highness. It was merely a question of tone. And, if I may add, they are men of not inconsiderable bulk."

The assayer, who was on the skinny side himself, looked around the room for sympathy.

"I could wish you had insisted on entry, nevertheless," said the king.

"Begging pardon, Your Highness, but perhaps if I had traveled with a guard—"

"Thank you. You may go." The king waved his hand.

The assayer ducked his head. "Your Highness, I have one further piece of information that may interest you. As I was preparing to leave, an individual of very large size approached me. Of immense size, this man was, such size as made his fellows seem—"

"Size noted," the king snapped.

"This man spoke not a word but led me behind the building in question, where there stood a kiln. And beside the kiln was a row of boots."

"Boots?" The king raised his eyebrows.

"Children's boots, by their appearance. The large man picked up a pair that might have fit a child of three or four, and tossed them on the fire. Then he walked away."

"And what do you assume from this?" asked the king.

"I make no assumptions, Your Highness. I merely relay facts."

But Annie knew what to assume. Hauler had wanted the assayer to know there were children at the Drop. And if Hauler wanted to help the other children, that meant . . . She felt a sudden surge of hope for Gregor and had to clap her hand over her mouth again to keep from grinning.

As soon as the assayer left, Page started to pace the short distance of the dais. Her gown swirled with every turn. Through Page's stockings Annie could see the bulge where the broken ankle bones had fused unevenly.

"Obviously Gibbet wasn't at any great pains to explain this away," Page muttered. "Even an imbecile would notice the mine chipping out twenty years ahead of schedule." She looked up. "Not that you're . . . I didn't mean . . ."

The king gave a tight smile. "Of course not. And you are correct about Gibbet. He must have known his smuggling would be exposed eventually, and the visit by the assayer has made the case plain." He looked at Annie. "He has known himself exposed for some weeks already. Miss Trewitt here escaped through his tunnel, after all."

"But he would never guess she'd come here!" Page exclaimed.

"He doesn't have to guess," Annie said.

"What do you mean?" The king's voice was sharp.

"He has an informant," she clarified. "Someone who—"

"Yes, I'm aware of what an informant is. Do you realize the gravity of the accusation you're making?"

Annie forced herself to meet his gaze. Her heart felt suspended high in her chest, the way it had after she and Gregor jumped from Quail Rock, hanging a moment in midair before plummeting into the river. She took a deep breath.

"The potion you use on the gardens to make the flowers bloom in winter, the potion you used on me, it's the same one Gibbet gives to the men at the Drop. And to the children."

The king opened his mouth, but she hurried on.

"The farm where Chopper caught me—the garden there is like this one, always in bloom. And the workers at the Drop all smell the same. They all smell sweet. I think if you give too much, it puts the person to sleep, but if you give just the right amount, they . . . they sleepwalk. They sleepwalk through everything, they don't complain, they don't try to run away. Chopper's garden is full of it, all the plants, so if you eat them you fall asleep, like I did. Either someone at the palace has passed the potion along to Gibbet without you knowing, or—"

"Or I sanctioned its use on the miners? Is that what you're suggesting?"

Annie stole a look at Page. She was gaping—literally gaping—at the king.

"Terrance?"

"The potion has been used to beautify the palace gardens since long before I was born. It was a gift to the first Terrance

Uncton from a friend and fellow surveyor. There is nothing dangerous about it."

Annie looked at the portrait on the wall behind them. "What was the name of the man who gave Uncton the potion?" she asked.

The king followed her gaze. A strange look came over his face, as though he wasn't sure whether to be frightened or pleased.

"Gibbet," he said. "The Gibbet family has been a friend of the crown for a long time. Until now."

"Then there is no informant." Page sounded relieved. "And the king would never allow that stuff to be used on the miners." She looked at Annie as if to say, *You see, he's not so bad.*

He sanctioned its use on me, Annie wanted to answer, but she didn't.

"Would it be so very bad if I had?" asked the king.

"What?" Page and Annie said at the same time.

"With the failure of the farms in the region, and the"—he spoke the next words rather quickly—"the incorporation of the fisheries, the people of Dour County may have found their opportunities for work somewhat curtailed. Would a man be so terrible to provide them something to make the difficult work of mining more palatable?"

Without a word, Page descended the dais and walked to the door.

"Would a man be so terrible?" the king called after her. "Would a man be unlovable, who did so?"

Page threw open the door.

"You are not excused!" the king bellowed.

She slammed the door behind her.

He raised his arm over his head. Annie felt a flash of panic and rage. But it was only, after all, to pull the tasseled rope that hung beside the throne.

⚬⚬

Annie caught up with Page outside the door to her room. Her sister's limp had been more noticeable coming up the stairs and even now, standing still, she shifted her weight from her bad leg to her cane. Watching her, Annie felt a sudden surge of love so strong she didn't know what to do with it. In the old days, she would have grabbed her around the waist and not let go. Now she took Page's hand in her own and simply held it.

"I don't want to stay here any longer," Page whispered.

Annie glanced up and down the hallway. "Together, with Sharta, we could leave," she said. "We could leave tonight! We'll need weapons, a map, food. Can he hunt for himself, do you think?"

Page was looking at her strangely.

"And lanterns! Of course we'll need lanterns. And plenty of matches and candles."

Page kept looking at Annie in that strange way. Then, slowly, she smiled. "You're mad, you know that?"

"You said Sharta wanted to warn his pack about Gibbet. So we'll do it! Then you and I can . . ."

"Storm the orphanage and rescue Gregor?"

"Well, why not?" Annie said hotly. "With Sharta . . ."

"Perhaps not Sharta alone."

"What do you mean?"

Page's voice turned brisk. "I'll get what we need. Be ready an hour after dark."

⁓⟋⁓

The fourth time she tripped over Prudence Annie bent down and scooped her up, slinging her over one shoulder like a stole. Already she was dressed in everything she owned. She had even polished her new boots, which needed polish about as much as the knick-knacks had needed dusting and the chairs straightening. She wished she had all those things to do over again. She tried the door, knowing it wouldn't budge. Page had locked her in before she left, in case anyone came by to check. Strictly speaking, she and Annie were both still prisoners of the crown.

At last the dark came. Fifteen, twenty, thirty-five, forty, fifty, fifty-five . . . at exactly sixty minutes past dark, a piece of paper appeared under the door.

It was a page cut from a book, a very old book. The lettering was curly and hard to read. A gold border ran around the edge of the paper. Thumbnail-size paintings of animals filled the margins. The title of the book was written at the top: *A Compendium of Creatures.* Below that were a big gold letter *B* and the words *Badger—Brightling.*

Badger, Barry Owl, Beaver, Bellaphel, Bittern. In the middle of the page was an entry somewhat shorter than the others.

Black Wolf: *(pl. wolves) Warm-blooded and carnivorous. Forest-dwelling. Similar in form to Frigian Ice-wolf, with pelt of black or russet hue. Largely nocturnal, vision exceptionally keen. Habits unknown. Much feared for its eerie cry. Common folk names: Witch's Wolf, Kinderstalk.*

In the margin was pictured the tiny, perfect likeness of a kinderstalk. It might have been Sharta, except with two bright dots of amber for the eyes. Annie turned the page over. On the back, where the black painted kinderstalk showed through the paper like a stain, Page had written a few lines: *It's time you knew their proper name. I'll be back for you. Don't hate me.—P*

࿔

After an hour the bone key cracked in her hand. Page had jammed something in the lock from the outside. An icy breeze touched Annie's damp skin, the back of her neck. *The window must be open,* she thought vaguely, and shivered. Then she raised her head: the window.

She could have picked a bouquet of flowers easily from where she sat on the sill, but this part of the vine was still new growth. The woody stem of the main plant clung to the palace wall several feet to her right. She would have to jump to reach it. Far below her the lawn glittered with frost beside vivid flowerbeds.

Isadore leapt onto the sill beside her, then onto the vine, easy as that. Prue followed him, stopping first to rub her cheek against Annie's knee. Annie looked down again, but this time she saw the yellow cliffs of the Drop, the river at the bottom of the gorge. She closed her eyes, as if that would keep her from seeing his face.

For Number Five, then. Do it for him.

She scooted to the farthest edge of the sill and crouched low on her haunches, as she had seen the cats do.

For Number Five. For Number Five. Don't look down. For Number Five. Jump!

Her body sailed through the darkness. Everything went quiet and for a moment she felt free and full of grace. Then she landed and got a face full of flowers, a fistful of leaves, a knee full of wall.

One backward, groping step at a time, she made her way down. The vine flexed under her weight and she couldn't help calculating how much heavier she was than the cats, how tiny were the actual fibers that held the plant to the wall.

She couldn't see the cats, couldn't see much of anything besides the green of the vine and the white stone of the wall behind it. Despite the cold, her eyes burned with the sweat trickling off her forehead. Every so often she would stop and lean out to see how far she was from the bottom. Each time, the lawn seemed just as far, the ladder of leaves just as high.

Still, she had to be getting close, and Page and Sharta couldn't be far ahead of her. The blind leading the lame, wasn't that the saying? Annie gasped as her foot slipped and she skidded a few feet down the vine. She supposed she deserved that.

She was about to take another step when she heard a strange noise above her. The sound was a creak and at the same time a whisper, like the sound a ship makes floating at dock. For a moment she was confused; she had the sensation of tipping backward, but she still had a tight hold of the vine. Then she understood.

The bindweed groaned as it loosed itself from the stone, one fingerlike branch after another snapping free. The top of the vine, already loose, had curved over itself like a question mark, its leaves hissing and whispering as they fell. She climbed frantically now, slipping more than climbing, her hands flayed by the rough stem, the hiss of the dying vine growing louder, chasing her, until the stem broke free under her hands and she plunged toward the earth.

And then she stopped falling, and began to bounce. Her hair flew up around her face, then fell back, then up again, then back. Annie found herself hanging upside down, her hands and feet hooked in a death grip around the stem. The vine bounced lightly a few more times, then stilled. The bottom part of the stem, the oldest, thickest part, had stuck fast to the wall. Annie twisted her head to the side, forcing herself to look down. Then she began to laugh, and cry. Not two feet from her face was the neatly trimmed, frost-tipped grass of the palace lawn.

❧

It was easy enough to slip past the guard. It was easy to do anything in the dark, people were so afraid. A handful of gravel on the flagstones of the courtyard, his quick turn and shout, her dash through the gates. She wondered how Page had managed it. Sharta? But the guard would have sounded an alarm by now. She watched him pat his breast pocket, then a moment later pat it again. Apparently the king's servants were easy to bribe.

At the bottom of the hill Isadore turned west, back along the Royal Way. When they reached the inn where she had stayed with Serena, Annie hesitated. Why would Page come here? But Izzy led her determinedly to the stable. She almost laughed when she saw him sitting beside a ladder lying lengthways on the ground, just beneath a square window near the roof.

But there was no trick here. The ladder led her right to the hayloft, and from there it was an easy climb down to the stable.

She followed Izzy past the drowsing horses to the last empty stall. Inside each stall was a water trough and a slatted wooden rack filled with hay. Izzy flicked his tail once, then squeezed between the slats of the hayrack. Prudence followed, reemerging seconds later with a piece of hay stuck in her whiskers. The rack was small and didn't look especially sturdy. And what if a horse was stalled here and began to eat? It was hard, sometimes, to trust a pair of cats.

Annie climbed into the rack and lay down, plucking fistfuls of hay to spread over herself. Her knees nearly touched her chin. She needed to sneeze. Her hands hurt where she'd scraped them on the vine. But the hay was new, and fragrant, and soft beneath her. No worse than her bed in the giant oak. Better by far than her bed at the palace.

Chapter 12

Again? We looked here already. I'm glad for the money, don't get me wrong, but it's insulting, looking for a girl."

Annie opened her eyes, instantly awake. Men. Big men in heavy boots and creaking leather gear. One of them was dragging the butt of something—a spear?—along the wall of the stable as he walked. *Thhhrrrd, thhhrrrd.* The noise stopped and she heard their voices again, very close by.

"Not just any girl. His betrothed."

The other man snorted. "If this was anything real he'd have the Royal Guard on it, not us."

"You didn't hear? Royal Guard's all gone. Sent them west late yesterday."

"For what?"

"'Liberate an orphanage.' Doesn't make sense to me either, but that's what the captain said."

So he's done it after all, Annie thought. She wondered if Page knew. "Ah, there's nothing here," the first man said. "Out all night in the dark? With a kinderstalk? She's dead. We all know it. *He* knows it. Let's get something to drink."

❧

The cats were waiting for her near the entrance to the barn.

"Let's go," Annie whispered.

Neither of them moved.

"What's the matter with you two?" And then she knew. Footsteps crossed the yard, the same as before—heavy and slow, accompanied by the clank of metal and the creak of leather. The air darkened as the men came into the barn, filling the doorway. There was no time to hide. They had seen her.

"Annie?"

Serena was wearing big boots, leading the horse into the barn by his halter. And behind her, tiny feet making no noise at all, came Beatrice.

❧

The twins made a seat for her in the back of the wagon with some grain sacks and an old horse blanket. Beatrice alternated between patting her arm and scolding her.

"Serena came home in such a lather when she found you gone! We've been back and forth across three counties. Don't tell me you've been in that stable all this time! But you look rather well. She looks rather well, doesn't she, Serena?"

"She looks our same Annie, which is to say somewhat mysterious and quite a dear. Now tell us, where are we going, and what are we about?"

Annie didn't know what to say. Then, looking at the two of them, an identical worry line drawn between their eyebrows, she did.

"I'm trying to find my sister. Will you help me?"

❧

If the twins thought there was anything unusual about the way Annie rode in the wagon—hunkered down almost flat, with a blanket over her head—they didn't say so. They chatted quietly together, only asking her from time to time if they were still headed the right way. Annie wasn't sure what the right way was, but her instincts told her to keep close to the forest.

"Go north," she said, and Serena drove north.

When they stopped to rest the horse, Annie watched Prue and Izzy chase some prey under the hedge at the side of the road. Winter was ending. A layer of dirty snow still covered the countryside, but the frost that had gripped the earth for months had begun to melt, making the road soft. Annie couldn't help smiling at the neat little trail of paw prints the cats left behind them.

The next instant she was down from the wagon and on her knees in the roadway. Clearly delineated in the mud were the heel and toe of a small boot and, a few inches ahead, the shallower impression of a foot that had touched the ground lightly. To the right of the footprints was a deeper print, round and perfectly symmetrical—the print of a cane.

"Serena, Bea, look! My sister came this way."

"That's wonderful, dear, just wonderful!" Bea called from the wagon. "Serena, did you hear what Annie said?"

Serena had climbed down from the wagon and stood frowning at the ground a few yards off. "A kinderstalk has been here. A large one, by the look of it."

The fat, splayed pads of an animal's foot were visible in the mud. A smaller indentation above each pad showed where the nails had dug into the earth.

"It crossed the road here, and then . . . oh my. Oh my goodness. Annie, don't—"

But Annie had already come up breathless beside her. "What? What is it?"

"Your sister's tracks and the kinderstalk's—I'm afraid they meet here. And it looks like . . . it looks as though only a single pair continues on."

Annie bowed her head. She was grateful her hair shielded her face, because she was smiling. Sharta had made those tracks. She knew it. It was almost as if she could smell him, his particular, shaggy scent, blood and pine.

"Oh, the poor dear!" Serena swept Annie into her arms and began to rock back and forth. Bea hovered around them like a hummingbird, darting in to touch Annie's back or stroke her hair.

"There, there, don't cry. We don't know for certain what's happened."

But Annie knew exactly what had happened. Page had gotten tired of walking and climbed on Sharta's back. Page was riding a kinderstalk! No, that wasn't right. Kinderstalk wasn't right. *It's time you knew their proper name.* Sharta was a wolf, a black wolf. And a wolf had carried Page to the palace. What had she said before she left? *Perhaps not Sharta alone.*

Annie wiggled free of Serena. "You're right, we don't know for certain what's happened. Let's keep going, can we?"

The sisters exchanged a look. Then Bea smiled with such kindness that Annie felt ashamed. "Of course we'll keep going. Of course we will."

❧

Night was approaching. They could all feel it, the way the blue air seemed to thicken. Beatrice wanted to find an inn, but for miles now they had seen nothing on either side of the road but lichen-covered boulders and bracka bushes. The straight black trees of the forest loomed in the distance.

The twins held a whispered conference in the front seat.

"Turn back to Millerville?"

"No time. Worse to be on the road."

"But the danger!"

"No sightings these six weeks."

"Well, I don't like it."

"I don't like it either. I don't like it one bit."

Serena turned to Annie with a forced smile. "We'll have to camp. But don't you worry. These days I travel prepared for every emergency."

They jolted off the road a few yards and parked in a field of boulders.

"Annie, would you see to the horse?" Serena said. "But don't tether him. If they—I want him to have a chance."

While Beatrice laid out the bedrolls in the back of the wagon, Serena walked swiftly among the stones, sprinkling something from a can at the base of each boulder. She returned to the wagon a bit winded, and sprinkled the rest of the liquid on the ground around the wagon wheels. Annie buried her nose in the sleeve of her cloak.

"Skunk musk," Serena said. "The kinderstalk hate it even more than we do." She wiped her hands on her dress and nodded approvingly at her sister. "That's nicely done, Bea."

Beatrice had prepared the beds and hung lanterns on every side of the wagon. It was a strange sight, the lanterns blazing in broad daylight, but even before Annie had completed the thought the sky changed to black. Serena gasped. Beatrice made a small, choked sound. She made the sign of protection three times, once in Annie's direction, once in Serena's, and once over her own heart.

"I'll take first watch." As she spoke, Bea reached beneath the wagon seat and pulled out a rifle. Then she reached under the seat again and took out a pistol, a second pistol, a cudgel, an ax, and finally, a burlap sack containing an assortment of knives. Some were short and beveled for jabbing, others long and thin for slicing.

Annie selected a short knife with a heavy handle that fit well in her palm. The blade was rounded, like a spear, and ended in a sharp point. She touched her finger to the tip and a drop of blood welled to the surface. Hastily Annie wiped her finger on her cloak and climbed back into the wagon.

Lying beside Serena in the darkness, Annie felt a strange kind of peace come over her. Despite the danger of their position, despite her worry over Page, there was something about the intense cold, the deep stillness of the night air that felt good to her. The hours crept by, and when Beatrice moved to nudge Serena awake to take her shift, Annie laid a hand gently on her arm.

"Let me, I'm awake already."

Beatrice looked at her questioningly. "Do you know how to fire a rifle?"

Annie shook her head. "I'll wake you if there's need. Don't worry."

Beatrice hesitated, but her fatigue won out. She took Annie's place beneath the warm covers and was asleep in seconds. Annie placed her weapons on the seat beside her and wrapped a blanket around her shoulders. She sat for a few minutes with the rifle across her lap as Beatrice had done, but she couldn't stand the feel of it so she laid it at her feet. All this time, the cats had not stopped moving, weaving in and out of the shadows as they prowled the perimeter of the boulder field.

First her nose and then her cheeks stiffened with cold. Her back ached from sitting straight for so long on the hard seat. The sharp scent of skunk musk hung over everything. She closed her eyes, just for a moment, and the sounds of the land at night filled her ears, the wind clicking through the bare branches of a bracka bush, the scuffle of an animal leaving its burrow, the shriek of a bird hunting, and somewhere to the west, the *blub-blub* of water issuing from the earth. A spring. In the morning she should remember to tell them.

Annie's head drooped toward her breast. Then, with a

gasp, she was wide-awake. There she was on the same hard seat, in the circle of lantern light. Serena and Beatrice still slept in the back of the wagon. A light snow had begun to fall, dusting the blankets that covered them. But it wasn't the snow that had wakened her. Annie sat very still, straining her ears. There was nothing to hear: all the animals had fallen silent. Even the wind had died down.

Annie slipped the knife into her boot. After a moment's hesitation, she picked up a pistol. She laid the rifle next to Beatrice and jumped down from the wagon.

The cats were beside her in an instant. Prudence kept bumping against her ankles, and Isadore would sit, stand, walk a few paces, and sit again. With a last, worried glance at Beatrice and Serena, Annie turned and began to walk north. The closer she came to the forest, the deeper the silence grew.

When the cry finally came, Annie realized two things at once: this was what she had been listening for, all along, and it was much, much worse than she could have imagined.

The cry went on and on, part howl, part scream, part sob, part snarl. Not wolf, not human, but both together. Page and Sharta. The pistol banged against her thigh as she ran. Light flickered ahead of her through the trees. The cries came intermittently now, but there were new sounds, grunting and scraping. Shapes emerged from the darkness, gigantic shapes, thrashing wildly in a violent dance. Annie stumbled, stopped. Those weren't wolves. They were monsters. It took her a moment to realize that she was seeing not the animals themselves, but their shadows, cast in huge relief on a boulder behind them. A large torch, planted in the ground, bathed the writhing bodies in light.

As she drew nearer, Annie recognized Sharta, his white eyes rolling in his dark head. He had the other wolf by the throat and was shaking him as hard as he could. The other wolf scrabbled at Sharta's neck with his claws, trying to reach the vulnerable veins of the throat through the thick ruff of fur that protected them. Both animals were bleeding freely from wounds on their torsos and flanks.

A few yards from where the wolves fought lay Page's cane. Like an arrow, it pointed toward the deep shadows on the other side of the boulder.

✦

The wolves had gathered in a semicircle, at least twenty of them. Page stood with her back pressed against the rock, her hands spread in front of her in a supplicating gesture. She was speaking rapidly in the sharp, broken tones of Hippa. The wolves seemed neither to hear nor understand her. A wolf with a reddish brown coat lunged forward, snapping and bark-ing. Page screamed and cowered against the rock. Another wolf leapt forward, snarling, then backed away.

"Stop!" Annie cried.

Page looked around wildly. "Annie? Is that you?" Fear chased hope across her face. "Get away from here! Go!"

At the sound of Annie's voice several of the wolves turned their heads. The red wolf looked her straight in the face. Slanted amber eyes ringed with black, the muzzle and shoulders narrower than Sharta's. A female, Annie realized. A beautiful animal.

She raised the pistol.

Something that had been alive in the wolf's face, some question, went dull. She barked twice and the pack broke apart, wheeling in different directions like a flock of startled birds. Annie stood frozen for a moment, struggling with a queer sense of loss.

"Annie, are you there? What's happening?"

"They're gone." She walked over to Page and touched her arm. Page jerked away, then jerked toward her, grabbing clumsily at her cloak, her hair.

"He protected me! He couldn't see, but he protected me. He saved me again."

∼✺∼

It reminded her of leaving the orphanage with Gregor, her sister's body a trembling weight, clutching Annie like a buoy in the darkness.

As soon as they reached the torchlight, Page broke away.

"Sharta! *Sharta!* Oh, stop it! Oh please, make him stop!"

The other wolf stood over Sharta as he writhed against the earth, his torso twisting in agony. His front claws scraped uselessly against the ground.

"Annie, please! Do something! Please, please help him!" Page was sobbing now.

A rush of different feelings struck Annie all at once. Pride at being asked for help. Fear and its tinny, resentful echo: why me? But mostly a sense of something being off, a kind of dread for what she was about to do. This was nothing like when she attacked Smirch or the king. This was deliberate.

She handed Page the pistol and took the knife from her boot. Up close, the wolves seemed impossibly huge. She edged up behind the standing wolf and raised her arm. *Don't do it. Not this way.* She plunged the blade into the meaty part of the wolf's hind leg. Instantly, he let go of Sharta. But she had expected him to cry, to fall. He whirled around and threw himself at Annie, knocking her to the ground. She smelled the stench of old wounds, the fresh blood. The wolf lowered his head. She gasped, and he stilled. Their eyes met. His eyes widened, then narrowed. He growled.

Their bodies were so close together that she felt the impact when he was struck once, then again. Izzy and Prue. The wolf snarled and lifted his head, trying to shake free the two small forms that clung to him, hissing and spitting. Relieved for a moment of his weight, Annie flailed around with her hands and feet, hoping some blow would land. Her foot knocked the handle of the knife still lodged in his leg, and the wolf yelped and leapt back. He twisted his head from side to side, a frantic gesture, and Annie realized he was looking for his pack. Again, she felt that queer pang of loss that they were gone. Felt it for him. She rolled sideways, away from the wolf, away from the feeling.

A change came over the wolf. He seemed to age before her eyes, to shrink and grow frail. His eyes gleamed dully and he stood for a moment, swaying, then fell, slow and heavy as a tree. He hit the ground with the whole weight of his life and lay still.

I killed him, Annie thought. *I killed a wolf.* She scrambled backward.

"Annie! Are you hurt? I couldn't . . . I don't know . . . and Sharta . . . I'm sorry! I'm sorry I'm so . . . *useless!* Let me look at you, let me help you!"

Annie grabbed her sister's wrists and gave her a little shake.

"Page, I'm fine. I'm safe."

Sharta lay crumpled in the snow, not far from the other wolf. His eyes leaked blood tears. Page knelt and took his head gently into her lap, stroking his ears and murmuring to him in Hippa. He growled weakly in response. Page raised her face to Annie.

"He's dying."

"No, Page, surely—I have a wagon; I'm traveling with two good women, strong women. We can help him." Page shook her head.

"It's too late; he wants to go. The wolf he fought was his son, Rinka." She said something else in Hippa and Sharta responded, weaker than before.

"He says we must try to save Rinka."

Annie looked at the wolf lying a few feet away. Snow was settling on his dark fur. She felt the tickle of blood on her neck where his teeth had grazed her.

Sharta's breath came in rattling pants. Page bent close to hear him.

"We must protect the pack, protect their future. Neither the king nor Gibbet will do it."

Annie studied the two faces, one stained with blood, the other with tears. She spoke in a clear, loud voice. "I will do whatever I can, Sharta."

Page whispered in his ear. Sharta tried to respond, but no sound came out. Page laid her hand over his wounded eyes and bent until her cheek rested on his breast. Then she buried her face in his fur and wept.

Chapter 13

Annie stood over the wounded wolf. The one Page had called Rinka, Sharta's son. Blood seeped from dozens of wounds and his injured hind leg lay at a strange angle. With the knife in one hand, poised to strike, she held her hand over his muzzle. Ragged puffs of warm air touched her palm. She lifted one of his eyelids. The white showed. Tentatively, she ran her hand over his side, from shoulder to flank. She could feel each rib, and his hipbones, even through the thick fur, were painfully sharp. She frowned. This wolf was emaciated. Stripping off her cloak, she wrapped it around his body, careful to protect him from the frozen ground. She went to Page and laid a hand on her shoulder.

"I'm going to get help. We have a wagon. You stay here." Page nodded without lifting her head. Annie put the pistol on the ground next to her sister and moved away.

"Annie, wait! Who is helping you? Can we trust them?"

"Yes." Annie hoped she sounded more confident than she

felt. People had strong feelings when it came to kinderstalk, even good people. Even the best people.

❧

In the end, she told them everything: about Uncle Jock and Aunt Prim, about Page and the king, about Gibbet and Sharta. She spoke quickly, staring at her lap, afraid that if she stopped or slowed down she wouldn't be able to start again. The twins listened without speaking. When she had finished and they still said nothing, Annie peeked up and found them staring at her, Beatrice in open-mouthed shock, Serena with an expression she couldn't read.

Gently, Serena gripped Annie's chin and turned her face toward her own.

"Yes, if you're wondering, I *am* angry with you, but only for not trusting us with this earlier. How can we protect you, protect *ourselves*, if we don't know what we're facing?" She sighed. "We knew you were in trouble, child, but nothing like this. We're a day's ride from home yet, but I'll see what I can do with the kinderstalk before then. Mind, you had better make sure it doesn't bite. And we'll have to use a blanket or some sort of covering; it won't do to go traipsing around the byways with *that* in the back of the wagon."

In a very small voice, Beatrice said, "Perhaps the kinderstalk can wear Mother's wig."

For a beat, they were all silent. Then Serena started to laugh. Her big belly shook. Annie laughed too, and it felt like water pouring from a burst dam.

She wiped her eyes. "Stop here."

The falling snow had obscured much of the wolves' blood, but still the women gasped and drew back at the sight of the two long black bodies.

Page had been sitting just as Annie left her, Sharta's head cradled in her lap. Now she rose and without a word to anyone began rolling rocks into a pile. Annie opened her mouth, a question on her lips, then closed it again.

Serena was crouched over Rinka, eyeing him closely.

"Doesn't weigh as much as he looks, I'll bet. Bea, come here and hold the jaws shut. Annie, drop the bed."

Annie stared at her, puzzled, until Serena jerked her head in the direction of the wagon seat. Level with the footwell was a wooden lever that Annie had never noticed before. She pushed the lever along its track and the back wall of the wagon bed fell flat. The bed tipped a few inches toward the ground. Serena eased Rinka's body onto the wagon. She washed his wounds with water from her canteen.

"Watch now, Bea," she said, and retrieved a needle and thread from her duffel bag. "It's really you who should be sewing this fellow up, not me. How anyone thought I could be a doctor with these sausage fingers . . ." She bent over the wolf, frowning in concentration. Beatrice tightened her hold on the muzzle. When she pierced the skin around the wound on his flank, Rinka jerked, nearly lifting Beatrice off the ground.

Serena chuckled. "That should teach you to eat a few more pancakes."

Bea glared at her sister. She held out her hand. "Let me, then. Maybe you won't be so fresh standing here by the thing's mouth."

~§~

Already Page had rolled several dozen rocks into a tight circle around Sharta's body. As Annie watched, she began to pile them on top of each other; the ground was still too hard to dig a proper grave. The two sisters worked side by side, building a tomb of rocks over the dead wolf.

Annie wished she had something to give him. Here, beyond the palace walls, the winter forest offered no flowers, no bright leaves.

But she did have something bright. From the pocket over her heart she took the lock of Page's hair. She handed it to her sister. "You give it to him."

Page opened the locket she wore around her neck and removed a coil of black hair. She braided it together with her own hair. She kissed the braid, then held it up for Annie to kiss.

"It's Mother's." She smiled, and tears ran around the corners of her mouth.

Annie smiled too, though she didn't understand why Page wanted to give Sharta their mother's hair. Together they placed the braid over the wolf's heart and rolled the last stones into place.

"I'm finished here." Beatrice's voice broke them apart. "There's not much I can do with the worst wound. Serena

thinks it's severed one of the tendons, so whether he'll walk . . ."
She gave a slight shrug. "Time will tell."

᭶

Around midmorning the snow started again and fell steadily
all day, a wet, heavy snow that soaked their clothes. Page sat
with Annie in the back of the wagon, her skirts pulled tightly
around her so that not even her cloak touched Rinka's body.
Occasionally, he would shudder or sigh and they would all
hold their breaths, but he remained in the deepest of sleeps.

When at last they rolled up to the twins' house, the air
tasted of nighttime and they were all cold, weary, and thoroughly miserable.

"Girls, why don't you start a fire and set out the supper
things," Serena said. "See what you can find in the pantry.
Between the four of us . . ." She looked over at Rinka, then at
the cats. "Between the *seven* of us, I imagine we'll just about
clean it out."

When neither Page nor Annie moved, she sighed, hands
on hips. "Listen, you two sprouts. I've seen more strange
things in my life than you can imagine. This ranks among
them, but it hasn't curled my hair yet. Now run along and get
supper going; I'm ready to devour the table and chairs without
salt."

They dined on flatbread and a hunk of very old, very pun-
gent cheese. Beatrice got up from time to time to tend a stew
bubbling over the fire. As they prepared for bed, Annie offered
to sleep on the hearth to keep an eye on Rinka. She thought

Page might object, but her sister followed Serena upstairs without a word. To the room with the bird quilt, no doubt.

Annie lay down with her back to the fire, facing the wolf. He smelled of fever. She closed her eyes. When she opened them again the fire had died and the room was cold. Rinka had rolled onto his stomach. He was panting and his eyes were bright.

Annie filled a bowl with the stew Beatrice had made, still warm in its iron pot. She slid the bowl across the floor with her foot. The wolf sniffed at it, whined, and turned his head away. Annie felt a stab of something like hurt.

"There's nothing wrong with it. You should eat. Look."

She picked up the bowl and lapped at the stew. The wolf kept his head turned away but his ears, she saw, had swiveled toward her.

"Mmmm, what delicious stew! How good it tastes! I think I'll eat it all up."

"Annie, what's going on?" Page stood at the foot of the stairs, looking like a child in one of Serena's nightgowns.

"Nothing. I was trying to get him to eat. I think he has a fever."

"Good. I hope he dies."

"Page! Sharta said—"

"I know what he said. But this wolf . . . you don't know anything about it, Annie."

"Then tell me!"

"Lower your voice!"

They glared at each other across the room. Page rolled her eyes and pointed to a chair.

"Sit down."

Annie sat. The wolf watched them out of his bright gold eyes.

"I am going to start two hundred years ago, with Howland's first king."

"Terrance Uncton."

Page looked surprised. "Yes."

Annie nodded, pleased with herself. "He discovered the first great cache of ringstone. The palace is built on top of the old mine."

"It is. But do you know what was there first, before the palace and before the mine?"

Annie's pleasure vanished. "Does this have to be question and answer?"

Page smiled a real smile. "Go get the almanac. I saw it in the kitchen. Bea appears to be using it as a stepstool to reach the sink."

When Annie returned, Page had spread a piece of paper out on the table. It was a map, an old map, drawn on the same soft yellow paper with the same gilt edges as the page from the *Compendium of Creatures*. One of the edges was furred where it had been torn from the binding.

Page followed her gaze. "It's awful to tear them up. But I couldn't carry the whole thing with me. And there are so many, many books in the Royal Library, Annie. So very many beautiful old books that no one reads."

Like most people, Beatrice and Serena kept maps at the back of their almanac. Page opened the map of Howland and laid it next to the old map.

"You see here, where Magnifica is today? Now look at this."

Annie followed her sister's finger to a pale circle in the middle of a vast, inky patch on the old map. Across the circle were written the words "Uncton Mine."

"What is all this black ink around the mine?"

Page tapped the map. The word was barely visible against the dark background, the letters blurred with age: *Dark-wood*.

"The forest, Annie. It was all forest. You see here, to the east of the mine? Most of that was sand and marsh. The ringstone was easy to find there, and mostly above ground. But the rest, all of this"—she trailed her finger over the map to the West Sea, marked by stylized waves and a monstrous-looking fish—"all of this was forest."

Annie chose her words carefully. "The wolves lived in Magnifica before the king. Before it was Magnifica."

"Yes. The miners needed roads to reach the coasts. They needed houses and shops. They built the palace and then the city. The forest was in the way of all that."

"And the wolves—they moved?" Annie looked at the one big dark patch still left on the modern map of Howland. Dour County.

"Most of them died. But yes, the survivors moved."

"But so did the mine! I mean the new mine, the Drop."

Page shook her head. "The Drop meant more roads and more people, but it wasn't so bad for the wolves. Better the cliffs than among the trees."

"Not better for Gregor."

"No. Not better for Gregor." Page took Annie's hand. "Annie, what I'm going to tell you now, you cannot tell anyone. Not Beatrice or Serena. Not Gregor when we find him. Do you understand?"

"I understand. I promise."

"There is one last cache of ringstone. There is more stone there than in Uncton's mine, more stone than at the Drop."

Something cold and certain settled in Annie's chest. Her eyes found the fist of land raised toward the northwest corner of the map. Still she asked, "Where?"

"Finisterre."

"Does Gibbet know about the ringstone there?"

"Sharta thinks he does. I told him what you saw, Gibbet speaking with the wolf. He thinks—he thought—that Gibbet has made a bargain with the wolves. He learns their language. He throws them food from time to time. In exchange they let him mine at night. Perhaps they've even promised to help him take the crown. Who knows what he's promised them. Of course the first thing he'll do when he's king is tear a path to Finisterre."

Annie shook her head. "It doesn't make sense. I don't understand why the wolves would agree to fight for him."

"They are starving, Annie. Their pups are dying. Think of the men who go to work for Gibbet at the Drop. Would any of them choose that life if they could help it?"

"But Sharta must have warned them. Why didn't they listen?" Annie said stubbornly.

"They should have. But Sharta . . . he and his mate did

something a long time ago that turned the pack against them. They don't trust him. Especially Rinka."

"What did they do?"

"They helped a human."

All the time they had been talking, the wolf had never taken his eyes from them. Annie met his gaze. He bared his teeth.

"How did Gibbet find out about the stone?" she asked. "Why would the wolves tell him?"

"I don't know. Sharta didn't know either. Perhaps he learned in the same way he learned to speak Hippa. Gibbet is not like other men."

Annie hesitated. "Does the king know about Finisterre?"

"He doesn't. He mustn't."

"Page?"

"Hmm?"

"How can we convince Rinka that Gibbet can't be trusted if Sharta couldn't?"

"We can't. Like I said, it would have been better if he died."

After Page went to bed, Annie lay for a long time watching the wolf. The shivering stopped at last. His eyelids drooped. When she was sure he was asleep she reached out and touched her finger to one black paw.

The wolf wanted to travel with Annie. Annie alone.

"Of course it's out of the question."

"But why, Page? I think we have an understanding, Rinka and I." Annie looked around hopefully for a nod from Beatrice or Serena, but they were studying the breakfast buns with rapt attention.

Page set down her teacup.

"And what understanding is that? That he'll use you for food and transport until he's well enough to kill you? Or perhaps he won't wait that long. Perhaps he'll call his pack the first night on the road and they'll do the killing for him. Is that what you understand?"

Annie's breath caught in a hitch of outrage.

"I'm sorry," Page went on. "But just because you've spent the past three days barking at each other across the hearth doesn't make you friends."

Rinka looked up from his bowl of stew. He was nestled comfortably in the bed Annie had made for him out of an old quilt.

"Rinka," Annie asked. "How do you say 'my sister is unpleasant' in Hippa?"

He cocked his head to the side and barked.

"Again."

This time she closed her eyes. The bark wasn't a single note, but an arc of sound, starting low, back in the wolf's throat, and ending high, behind his teeth. *What do you ask?*

Carefully, eyes still closed, she barked back. *I ask how say sister bad.*

He made a sound that could only be a laugh. Annie opened her eyes to find Page struggling between expressions of surprise and annoyance.

"You've made considerable progress," she said primly.

Annie leaned across the table. "Page, just listen a moment. The king is looking for you. I heard his soldiers talking at the inn the day after we left the palace. Disguise yourself all you want, you still look . . . the way you look. He doesn't care about me. I'll hide Rinka in the back of the wagon. May we borrow it, and the horse?" Beatrice nodded vigorously without looking up from her plate. "And I'll stay on my guard around the wolf. I promise."

"And if you do reach his pack, what then?"

"I'll talk to them. I'll practice Hippa every day. I'll tell them what Gibbet really wants, what he'll do to Fin—" She caught herself. "I'll warn them of the danger. We have to try, Page. Sharta told us to try."

Page dropped her head between her hands and rubbed her temples. Annie took the opportunity to cast beseeching looks at Serena.

"It *is* dangerous," Serena ventured. "And I don't like our Annie to go alone any more than you do. But if this Gibbet is planning something as bad as you say, perhaps the risk is well run. None of us wants to get caught in the middle of a civil war." She glanced uneasily at Rinka. "Especially not with an army of kinderstalk."

"Not that we'd dream of interfering in a family dispute," Bea put in, looking significantly at Serena.

"Not dream of it," Serena replied.

The fight left Page. She slumped in her seat. "I promised Father I would keep you safe."

"I was a baby then."

"Why won't you let me keep you safe?"

"I can go?"

"I hate it. But yes, go."

⊰⊱

The rest of the day passed in a frenzy of preparations. Page and Annie ran around gathering supplies; Serena hammered away at the wagon, alternately cursing and coaxing it into shape for a long journey; and Beatrice disappeared in a cloud of steam and flour in the kitchen. Hours later she emerged with strips of salted fish and pork, jars of buttermilk, red, wizened links of sausage, flatbread, leeks, endless oatcakes, and the last of the fresh meat from the icebox.

She wagged her finger at Annie. "Keep it packed in snow as best you can. And make sure he doesn't eat it all at once or he'll be sick."

⊰⊱

Annie and Page were in the barn getting the horse's tack together when Page tugged the end of Annie's braid. "Look at me."

Reluctantly, Annie raised her eyes. She dreaded the hardness she would find in her sister's face. But Page surprised her.

"Little one," she said, stroking Annie's hair away from her forehead. "Besides you, Sharta was my only . . ." She bowed her head. "I'm only letting you go because I know, we both know, you'll go anyway."

She pulled Annie into her arms, squeezing her tight. Annie's ear was crushed against one of the ornate buttons on Page's cloak, but she didn't mind.

She spoke into her sister's shoulder. "Bea's calling. To feed us again, probably."

Page laughed and let her go. "Then let's eat."

But when Annie made to leave the barn, Page hung back.

"Wait. There's something else." She had an odd expression on her face, as though she was nervous but not about to admit it.

"The other night, when Sharta died, how did you find me?"

"What do you mean? You could hear the fighting a mile away."

Page shook her head. "No, I mean, how did you *find* us? It was night and you didn't have a torch—how did you even know what direction to walk? That night you found me in the pleasure forest—you didn't have a light then either."

Annie felt the smile stiffen on her face. It seemed unfair that Page should ask her this, but Annie wasn't sure why she resented it. She wasn't even sure why she hadn't told Page about her dark sight.

"I did have a torch. You must not have noticed," she lied.

Page looked confused. "But you were holding the pistol in one hand and I'm sure you—"

Beatrice appeared, flapping a dishrag at them from the doorway. "Girls! I've been calling you! Supper is nearly cold."

They'd agreed Annie should leave after breakfast the next day. Bea had baked a dozen dandelion muffins. Serena had plotted her course.

"If you travel hard you'll reach the Wren's Nest Inn before dark. Mistress Zeb that runs it is an old friend of mine from my trips west. Tell her I sent you. She'll help you see to the wagon. Best not show her what's *in* the wagon, mind," she added hastily. "But she won't pry."

Annie nodded and smiled and studied the map, but she had no intention of doing any of it. Despite what she'd told Page, she felt fairly certain the king's soldiers would be on the lookout for her, too. And Gibbet's men—she could just imagine Smirch knocking on the door of the inn. *Seen our girl? Long hair? About so tall? Keep your eyes peeled. There's stone in it for whoever helps us find her. We do miss our girl. We surely do.*

She would travel at night. She would be invisible.

The note contained a lie, but only a small one.

Dear Page, Beatrice, and Serena,

We left at dawn. I couldn't sleep in any case, and didn't see a reason to wake you. I have my map and my muffins. I will find some way to send word when I have news.

My love to you all,
Annie

They set out in the perfect dark. Whatever feeling of change or wonder the dawn brought, the dark evoked its opposite. How long had they been on the road? Ten minutes? Forty? Annie felt she had always been exactly here, on this hard seat, staring between the horse's fringed ears, and always would be. It wasn't a bad feeling. The dark seemed full of patience, full of peace. The wolf dozed in the back amid sacks of food, a blanket pulled up under his chin as if he were a child. The cats slept beside her on the seat.

Chapter 14

At the first sign of dawn they turned north to travel the few miles across country to the forest. Baggy balked at leaving the road, but Annie coaxed him into it without too much trouble.

"Apples, Baggy, as soon as we get there, with sugar on them."

She had forgotten how dark the forest was in daylight, how long it held the night sky with its million branches. The pleasure forest on the palace grounds was no more like this forest than a lap dog was like a wolf, she thought, and wondered how Sharta had been able to stand it.

Page. Page had helped him stand it. Annie glanced back at Rinka, alert now and sniffing the air. Could they trust each other, as Page and Sharta had?

"Whoa, Baggy."

They stopped in a clearing just wide enough to turn the wagon around. The horse's muddy hooves made dark circles in the snow covering the forest floor. She'd been glad for the start of warmer weather, but she shouldn't have been. The road held their tracks like a mold.

Rinka swallowed his food listlessly. She tried to examine the wound in his leg, but he snarled and jumped from the wagon bed, landing clumsily chest-first in the snow. He tried a few times to walk, but each time he fell it seemed to take a greater and greater effort to get up. Finally he stayed down, turning his head away from her.

As Annie was arranging the blankets for her bed, she caught sight of Isadore washing himself. He had kicked up one hind leg above his ear and was cleaning the fluffy white fur of the under-side. In that position, his leg appeared to be caught up in a sling. Annie jumped down from the wagon and hurried over to Rinka. She tore a wide band of cotton from her petticoat and knelt beside him. He didn't look at her. She touched his leg; he jerked away from her, growling. To her surprise, Annie growled back. Now Rinka did look at her, his ears cocked in surprise.

"I'm just trying to help you," she muttered.

If a wolf could shrug, Rinka did. He laid his head on his paws and looked into the distance with a bored expression, but when she touched him again he didn't pull away. Care-fully, she worked the piece of cotton around his hips and then around the second joint of the injured leg, tying it close to his body so only the tips of his toes were visible. As she worked, she spoke to him softly in her own language, telling him what she was doing and why she thought it would help. He shifted his weight from side to side as she passed the cloth under him and yapped at her when the bandage felt too tight.

Sitting back on her heels, Annie eyed her handiwork. The white cotton stood out starkly against his dark fur. Annie giggled. She couldn't help it—the bandage looked like a giant diaper. She laughed harder, until she rocked back and landed on her elbows in a mist of snow. Rinka narrowed his eyes.

"You, baby. Person baby," Annie tried in Hippa. She must have said it correctly, because he glared harder.

"How say, 'ha-ha-ha'?"

The Hippa sound for laughter drove the humor straight out of her. Like a rusty hinge, or a bone breaking.

Annie ate her breakfast and pretended not to watch Rinka's attempts to walk in the diaper. He fell over, once, twice, a third time, but on the fourth try he stayed standing. He hopped a few paces, stopped to steady himself, then hopped a few paces more. By the time Annie had settled under the blankets he was moving quite quickly around the copse of trees where they had made their camp.

"I take sleeps now," she called out.

The wolf turned his head and looked at her quizzically. She cleared her throat and tried again, laying more emphasis on the first syllable of the bark: *I take sleeps now.*

This time his ears perked up and he barked back: *Sleep soundly, dark hair.*

∼§∼

Annie dreamt of wolves. Dozens of them ran over the white earth. One wolf began to fall behind the others. He limped on three legs, then began to crawl, not a wolf anymore, but a baby. Behind them, out of the trees, came a laughing black bird. The bird swooped down and snatched up the child. All the wolves began to howl.

Annie sat up, heart pounding. Far off, she could hear Rinka howling for his pack. No answer came, and after a long time she heard his scuffing gait return to camp. She lay down, but did not sleep again.

❧

The second night of their journey passed much as the first, the darkness unspooling itself slowly as they made their way along the wide, rutted road that linked east and west Howland. Annie practiced speaking Hippa to the horse, but it was hard to engage a pair of hindquarters. Rinka, exhausted from his attempts at walking, scarcely moved. Gradually the road turned south to accommodate the growing bulk of the forest. They had entered Dour County.

❧

"Leave the road. Quickly."

Annie started. She had dozed off. Light filled the sky to the east.

Blushing, hoping the wolf hadn't noticed, she turned the wagon north.

"Soon Finisterre," she said in Hippa. "Tomorrow, or—"

"Be quiet."

Annie turned in her seat, mouth opened in protest. The wolf

lay hunched against the wagon bed, head and ears straining toward the empty road.

"What is it?" Annie whispered.

"Listen."

She closed her eyes and tried to quiet her heartbeat and her breath.

Koom, koom, koom.

The sound broke in two, the beat followed by the echo of the beat.

Koom-koom, koom-koom, koom-koom.

Hoofbeats.

The sound splintered into fragments: creak of leather, slap of reins, spatter of mud, grunting breath.

She opened her eyes. A dark cloud stood out against the brightening sky, moving fast. Annie shook the reins. "On, Baggy, on!"

To her astonishment, the old carthorse broke into a smooth, powerful canter. The wagon jumped and bumped over rocks and ditches. Annie looked back. She could make out the sharp points of spears now and the glint of armor. Soldiers, and not mercenaries this time.

The forest loomed ahead of them, a haven. Even if the King's Guard dared to follow them, they could split up. They could hide among the trees.

Only about fifty yards left, forty . . . the horsemen swerved from the road and pounded toward them.

Twenty yards. They were closing the distance to the forest. They were going to make it.

Then, with a great crack, the wagon tipped sideways.

Annie screamed and gripped the seat. In a blur of orange, she saw Isadore's body flying through the air, then she felt her own fingers come loose and realized that she, too, was flying.

She landed hard. Snow filled her ear. She struggled to a sitting position and found herself looking into the flared black nostrils of a horse. Something caught hold of the back of her cloak and she was lifted onto her feet.

"Are you injured?"

Annie raised her eyes past the horse's broad chest. The horse was twice the size of Baggy. Its coat was the color of smoke. The man holding her cloak looked like an extension of the horse. His nostrils flared big and black and a bushy gray beard obscured most of his face. Behind him four more men waited on horseback. They were all broad and bearded, except for one who had no hair at all. The skin hung in triple folds around his neck, like the neck of a turtle.

"The captain asked if you were injured," the turtle said.

She shook her head, peeping around as she did so for the others. Rinka and the cats were nowhere in sight. The wagon lay on its side, three remaining wheels spinning slowly. Baggy stood trembling between the snapped shafts.

The captain surveyed the supplies scattered over the ground: apples, blankets, candles, spoons, even Bea's muffins.

"You're a tradesperson of some kind, I gather?"

Annie hesitated. "Yes. Yes, I am."

"Produce your travel permit, please."

"My permit. Of course." She pretended to search her pockets, casting around all the while for something she could use to—what? One of the horses kept tossing its head. On the ground by its feet were a carrot, a rye loaf, and there, in a red lump, the meat Beatrice had packed for Rinka.

"Oh, thank the dawn!" Annie cried. "My employer would have skinned me alive if I'd lost this."

"Lost *that?*" the captain asked.

"Oh, yes. He's a very cruel man, my employer." She raised her eyes in what she hoped was a pathetic expression. "He's a butcher."

The captain looked taken aback.

"I'm wondering why she ran when she saw us, Captain," said the turtle.

"Specialty meats!" Annie blurted. "This here is, is . . . *barn owl, bellaphel, bittern* . . . Bittern! Bittern meat, imported from Brineland. Worth its weight in ringstone. That's why he makes me travel so early. So we won't be robbed. I ran because I thought you were robbers."

The captain looked over at his fellows, who shrugged.

"We still need to see her permit, Captain," the turtle said. "We can't let her go without seeing that permit." He was nearly standing in his stirrups with eagerness. Annie wrinkled her nose. The men smelled of sweat, leather, ale, horse, and, from one of them, an unmistakable, tinny sweetness. Annie took an involuntary step back, only to find her cloak still caught in the captain's grip.

He turned on the turtle impatiently. "I'm more than capable of conducting this interview myself, Remo." Then to Annie, "Your permit, Miss."

Annie shook her head.

"You'll have to come with us then, I'm afraid."

"But why? I told you, my employer . . ."

"Strict orders from the king himself." As he spoke, the captain leaned down and hooked his free hand under Annie's arm.

"No! I won't!" But she had barely started to struggle when a black shape hurtled toward them.

"Kinderstalk!" one of the men yelled, and everything burst suddenly into chaos.

"Run!" Rinka snarled, just before his teeth closed around the captain's arm.

Annie ran, slipping and stumbling in the snow, afraid to look back. She heard shouting, a horse's frightened whinny, and then pistol fire.

Rinka, Rinka. What have you done?

She burst into the shelter of the trees and dropped to her hands and knees. But someone was behind her, drawing close. She scrambled up, ready to run again. Rinka's teeth nipped her shoulder.

He moved fast on three legs. At last they stopped.

"You are safe?" Annie panted. "No hurt?"

"No hurt."

"The others hurt?"

"The soldiers?" Rinka looked surprised. "Nothing serious."

Annie nodded, relieved. "They know now, about us. They tell the king."

"Certainly."

"But my sister! They say, 'a girl and kinderstalk.'" She said the word in her own tongue but Rinka's flattened ears showed he recognized it. "The king think Page and Sharta."

"What of it?"

"I do not know." Annie said. "But I fear . . . he look hard now for Page. And I think Gibbet man hide with soldiers. How say—spy?"

"Yes. More danger."

A crashing noise from the trees made Annie start. "Someone comes!"

A moment later Baggy trotted into view, still hitched to the cart shafts and trailing an uprooted bracka bush behind him. Prudence and Isadore slipped between his legs and came to rub against Annie's ankles.

"Poor Baggy!" She couldn't help smiling. Then she glanced at the path he had torn through the wood. "Men follow?"

Rinka bared his teeth in a grin. "Men forget how to count when it comes to wolves. One becomes four. Four become twenty. 'The monsters were everywhere!' they will tell the king, and they will believe it." His expression grew thoughtful. "This is what Gibbet understands that other men do not. Those soldiers you fear have fears of their own. He will give those fears form." Rinka shrugged. "Even if they do follow, it no longer matters. We will reach my pack long before they reach us."

Annie nodded, though Rinka's words were not quite what she'd call comforting. She finished unhitching the horse and planted a kiss in the middle of his long nose. Then she stooped and gave each of the cats a good scratch around the ears. Scattered, then reunited.

"I feel happy we . . . ," she began.

But the wolf had already moved off.

⤳

It was slow going, this walk through the woods. Snow filled Annie's boots with every step. Baggy, accustomed to the world of roads and fences, followed her so closely that his chin nearly rested on her shoulder. Annie practiced questions in Hippa to take her mind off her cold feet.

Where do we find the pack?

Do we go to Finisterre?

Do we look for Gibbet?

This last she must have spoken aloud. Rinka's ears swiveled toward her and he barked a reply.

"What do you say?" she asked carefully.

"I said yes. Gibbet and the wolves will be together."

"Do we look at the Drop?"

"No."

"At Chopper's farm?"

"No. Not there."

"Where do we go?"

"Follow me."

"I will follow you!" Annie skipped a few steps in the snow. It seemed to her that they weren't so much talking as collaborating in a magic trick. The wolf language, once a confusing tangle of sounds, had assumed rhythm and logic. She looked at the cats thoughtfully, and at Baggy. Surely if you could learn the language of wolves, you could also learn to speak to cats, to horses, to bugs even. Walking through the woods then would be like walking through a crowded market, hundreds of conversations going on at once. But perhaps ignorance of other species' languages was what kept things running smoothly. Would a wolf eat a rabbit, or a man shoot a deer, if they could speak to one another?

And now that she could speak to the wolves, would they listen? Would they believe her when she told them that Gibbet wanted to mine the ringstone at Finisterre? She had to try.

"Rinka! Slow down. I have something to tell you."

He stopped so abruptly she nearly tripped over him. They had reached a dense thicket. Bracka bushes strangled the oaks and reached their knotty fingers across the spaces between them, twining together until they formed a wall of brambles. The wolf looked different here somehow, wilder, rougher, as though he had grown out of the earth from the same dark roots as the bushes that surrounded him. Annie felt her heart beat a little faster.

"Rinka?"

He didn't answer.

"Rinka? What is happening? What are we doing here?"

Abruptly he turned on her, snarling.

"What are *we* doing here? *I* have come home. *I* am going to lead my pack into war. As for you? I couldn't have gotten here without you, and for that I won't tear out your throat.

But this"—he jerked his head toward his damaged leg. "For this I have you to thank, so don't test my patience."

The cats backed away from him, hissing.

"Rinka, what—"

" 'Rinka! Rinka!' " he sneered, imitating her. "Do you want to be a wolf, is that it? Looked around the human world and found you didn't have much of a pack?"

Tears burned in Annie's throat. She shook back her hair.

"And what sort of pack do you have? I see no one here but me."

The fur rose at the back of the wolf's neck. "You don't know anything."

"I know more than I did. I know now why your pack left you, why they never looked for you. I know what kind of—"

"Person I am?" he finished for her.

"Wolves have honor," she spat. "Sharta had honor."

"Sharta loved a human girl. There is no honor in that."

"And yet you would trust this human who is no more than a monster! Why?"

"Gibbet wants the throne and he needs us to secure it. In exchange he leaves us our little plot of land. How he treats his fellow men means nothing to me."

As they spoke, Rinka began to circle her slowly. With a kind of wonderment, Annie felt herself crouch, then drop to all fours. She lifted her nose to the air, suddenly aware of a tumult of smells. *What is happening to me?*

Rinka moved gradually inward, tightening the circle. She moved with him.

"Gibbet only cares about ringstone. Two things stand in his way: the king, and the wolves who guard Finisterre. He wants to destroy you both, Rinka. He will use you to destroy each other."

Nothing changed in the wolf's face. He made no sign that he had even heard her. But almost imperceptibly, his tail lowered.

She plunged on. "You know honor, Rinka! You didn't have to help me when the king's guard came. Show me that Page was wrong about you, Rinka."

"Stop saying my name."

"Rinka," she said again. "Rinka. Rinka. Rinka."

The wolf's muzzle pulled away from his teeth. His ears flattened against his head. Annie felt a creeping sensation at the top of her own skull, as though an invisible hand were pulling her hair back.

She smelled fear, rage, something that might have been regret. And then something else. Onions.

A man's voice reached them through the veil of brambles. Just two words, but his odor, the sound of his footfalls, the particular wheeze of his breath, all identified him as clearly as if he had been standing beside her.

"Their condition?" Gibbet asked.

"Starved, sir."

That was Chopper. Gibbet and Chopper. Blindly Annie reached out and found Prudence, close and comforting as always. Beneath her soft fur the cat's body felt tense as a bow.

The men stopped just beyond the hedge of bracka bushes.

"Then we're ready to send the first wave," Gibbet said. "No more than two hundred."

"So few, sir? The king's standing army alone is four times that number. As for mercenaries—"

"Two hundred kinderstalk, Chopper. It'll be the worst thing these men have ever seen. But the king's army is well trained. They'll stand and fight. They'll cut down the two hundred fast enough. Weary but triumphant, they'll begin to collect themselves. And then the second wave."

"The full eight hundred?"

"All of them. The king's troops will fall. Then it's up to the mercenaries and the farm boys used to shooting at the sides of barns."

"I underestimated you, sir."

"Not at all. You're just thinking like an old soldier. But we don't want this battle over with quickly, do we?"

Annie could hear the smile in his voice, could imagine the face split in two, the awful teeth.

"'Mass the dead, sir," Chopper said.

"'Mass the dead."

After a beat Chopper asked, "Assuming there are survivors among the kinderstalk?"

"That's a dirty job. Pip can do it."

"Thank you, sir."

"Now catch me up on the movements of our good King Terrance III."

"The king rode out three days ago. Apparently he plans to lead his own troops."

Gibbet laughed. "Better and better. How many men in his personal guard?"

"Can't say for sure. The Royal Guard is split up and riding all over the west, looking for his sweetheart that's run away with the blind kinderstalk. Couldn't have timed it better if she'd asked us."

Gibbet grunted. "And our own little runaway?"

The hair stood up on Annie's neck. For the first time, Chopper sounded nervous.

"Remo says the Guard had her but she got away. Says she has a kinderstalk with her, too."

"Two sisters, Chopper, light and dark. And neither comes to harm by the kinderstalk. Quite the opposite, in fact."

"The dark girl—you're sure she's Jock's younger daughter?"

"Not daughter, Chopper. The girls are orphans."

"Either way, sir, we found no mark. You said the child we wanted would bear a white mark."

Gibbet's voice turned ruminative. "Orphans, Chopper. Orphans belong in an orphanage. But Jock's wife said no, insisted on raising them herself. Fine, I told Jock, but you'll have to pay for the privilege: two stones at the end of every month, one for each girl. The older child kept to the house, but one day I saw her through the window. All that white hair. I wondered, could it be the mark? But we lost her. And then the younger one, just a child like any other child, easy to ignore, easy to forget. I should have drowned them both like a pair of kittens the day their father died." He paused. "It was a mistake, Chopper. A bad mistake."

"What was, sir?"

"Small greed. It rarely serves a man's larger ambitions. Remember that."

"Yes, sir."

"Tell the fool I'm ready to see him."

❧

They heard the scratch and flare of a match. Smoke rings rose above the hedge and broke apart on the lower branches of the trees. Through the bloom of tobacco Annie caught a new scent, mingling with Gibbet's stale odor of onions. Blood, and not human.

A sudden instinct made Annie turn to Rinka. He was gone. And then she saw him, creeping along the base of the hedge, searching for a break among the branches.

He is going to kill Gibbet. So let him, part of her said, even as she lunged after the wolf. Then Page's voice, a clear bell of warning: *Gibbet is not like other men.* Her fingers closed around a bony knob, a fistful of rough hairs. She had him by the tail.

To Rinka's credit, he didn't cry out. He moved forward a few steps, dragging Annie behind him. She relaxed her body into dead weight. For a moment they continued this strange, silent dance, Rinka advancing, Annie hanging back.

The wolf turned then and deliberately, in perfect silence, took Annie's leg between his teeth. There was no pain at first, just four clear points of pressure on her calf. He bit down. She pinched his tail. They both froze.

The footsteps were those of a tall, heavy man.

"You sent for me?" said Uncle Jock.

Chapter 15

If she hadn't been so close to Rinka, if their very teeth and nails hadn't connected them, she might have run. As it was she lay there and listened to her heart race on without her. The cats pressed against her back.

"You're a man who loves his weapon, aren't you, Jock? A good shot?"

Uncle Jock must have nodded. She could picture him, sly and afraid, nodding his head right off his shoulders.

"You see that bird with the red tail? Can you hit it?"

"The hawk? Sure."

The report came swiftly, then the bird's cry. Annie felt Rinka flinch.

"Wily bird. But close enough. Your girls can't fly."

"My girls are dead."

"Is it ghosts, then, bringing the king my news? Making friends with the kinderstalk?"

Uncle Jock didn't answer. He smelled damp: sweat and whisky.

"Girls, ghosts. It won't matter much longer," said Gibbet. "You owe me this, at least."

"But where do I find them? They could be anywhere in Howland! They—"

"The king will find the older girl. Why not start with her?"

"You mean the battle. You want me at the battle."

"You'll make a fine sniper, Jock."

"And that's all, that's all you want from me? The two girls?"

"Proof of kill. Then we're finished."

❧

Annie forced herself not to move for a full minute after they left.

She sniffed the air. "They're gone."

"They're gone," Rinka said at the same time. He sprang at her, not fierce, but frantic.

"What did they say? What has happened to the pack? That blood, that blood on his hands! My mate, Brisa. That is her blood."

Annie told him what she had overheard. She spoke without quite looking at him, afraid her face would betray what she was feeling. *Sharta was right. Page was right. Why didn't you believe us?*

At last she met his eyes. "We must track the first wave of wolves to the battle. We must try to stop it."

"No. First we find Brisa."

"Two hundred lives, Rinka! And my sister. If the king finds her she will be in danger."

"You may go alone. I won't stop you. But I must find my mate."

She had never thought of him as either old or young, and now he seemed both at once. Hopeless, full of hope.

"And when we find Brisa, you'll help me? You'll help me try to stop this war?"

"I'll do everything I can."

As far as she could see in either direction, the bracka hedge ran dense and toweringly high. Rinka sniffed along the base, looking for a way through. Annie snapped off one of the black-green leaves. It shriveled in her hand. This hedge was no accident of nature. Even here, even in the forest, Gibbet worked his potions. But the hedge gave Annie an idea. She broke off a bit of stem crowded with thorns, then tore a strip from the hem of her white petticoat. Then she pricked her thumb and, with blood as ink, wrote a message on the cloth.

King danger hide love

She clicked softly with her tongue. The cats appeared before her, their eyes fixed calmly on her face. She tied the strip of cloth around Prue's neck.

"Go find Page. Do your best to warn her. Tell her . . . tell her I'll come as soon as I can." Prudence rubbed her cheek against Annie's palm. Izzy flicked his tail. Then they were gone.

Annie stood abruptly, squinting against tears. Rinka was waiting for her perhaps fifty yards away. A small gap showed in the hedge. Through it she could see the flickering lights of Gibbet's camp. The lights multiplied as she watched—they were lighting the torches. Dark would fall soon.

Rinka plunged through the hedge. Thorns tore at his coat. Annie knew what they would do to her skin, but there was no other way.

"Baggy." She laid a hand on his neck. "You stay here, or go home, if you like. I'm sorry we can't—" Dark fell in the middle of her speech. Annie gasped and tightened her fingers in the horse's mane. And the horse, it seemed, had no intention of being left alone. He pushed past her and straight through the hedge. Brambles broke off in his mane and raked his sides. But Baggy was a workhorse and his hide was tough. Annie followed him through the gap, now wide as a door.

She could see the camp plainly now. Wolves, hundreds of them, milled around, their black bodies moving in and out of the shadows. A group of armed men stood near a cluster of tents. Torches blazed in a circle around them. As she watched, a wolf moved close enough to the circle to be seen by the men; one man gave a shout and another fired his pistol overhead in warning. "Stay in tight, men, stay in tight," someone said.

Chopper stood slightly apart from the others. Pip moved restlessly between an iron pot in which something was cooking and a tent-covered wagon at the edge of camp. A flap of red flesh hung over one eye. He stopped to stir the pot, frowned, peered inside, and stirred it again.

Another wolf moved into the light, just the tip of its tail, just for a second, but there came the shout and warning shot. In the brief hubbub that followed, Pip caught Chopper's arm and drew him aside. Annie crept into the shadowed space between the covered wagon and the tent closest to it.

"What do you mean not ready?" Chopper asked. He sounded impatient.

"No, no, they're ready, all right, it's just . . ."

"What?"

"It's nothing, except, well, they've rotted through the bags."

"And?"

"The apothecary said they'll eat them, but it doesn't . . . it looks just awful, Chop, and it smells worse. I don't see how they will. And whatever that is in the pot, it won't begin to cover it."

"When did they feed last, Pip?"

"Two days ago now."

"And how long yet before they feed again?"

"Until they return from the fight. Unless . . . unless they eat the—"

"They've been ordered not to."

"Right."

"So, Pip?"

"Yes, Chopper?"

"They'll eat them. And, Pip?"

"Chop?"

"I'd listen to the apothecary."

Pip nodded, abashed, but he didn't look convinced. He covered his nose and mouth with his shirttail and stepped inside the tent. A moment later he reappeared, stumbling backward. He held his hands in front of him as if to ward off danger.

"Beg pardon! Beg pardon! I didn't know you were inside!"

A small bent figure followed him out, leaning on a heavy

wooden staff. The figure shuffled forward, stabbing with its staff at Pip's legs and anyone else who stood too close. When it reached the cooking pot the figure straightened up a little and the hood fell back. Annie gasped.

She couldn't tell if she was looking at a man or woman, an aged person or a child. A few wisps of hair clung to a pointed head, and huge, beautiful eyes protruded slightly from a sallow face. The features were delicate, the mouth a red bow. The figure muttered something Annie couldn't hear, then shook a handful of glittering grains into the pot. She—for Annie had decided it must be a she, to have such a face—dipped her staff into the pot. As she stirred, a foul-looking blue smoke rose from the brew. But the smell that reached Annie was delicious: warm, spicy, sweet, savory, all at once. The apothecary breathed deeply, closed her eyes and nodded. Then she smiled. The bow-shaped lips, a child's mouth, parted to reveal row after row of pointed black teeth. The smile seemed to split her whole head in two, as though she would turn herself inside out. More than Chopper or Gibbet, more than Uncle Jock, this woman, this *creature*, terrified Annie. A trickle of dark fluid slipped from the corner of her mouth and ran over her chin before it dropped, glistening, into the pot. Pip's eyes widened with horror. The apothecary hooted with laughter, then drew up her hood and hobbled back into the tent.

❦

Rinka nudged Annie's shoulder. "I've found the break in the hedge they're using for an entrance. But Brisa—"

He stopped speaking midsentence, transfixed by the blue smoke rising over the fire. The other wolves, too, had gone strangely still. Their heads were all turned toward the smell, their noses testing the air. Even the men, the men who must have known better, began to saunter over to peer into the pot. Annie's mouth filled with saliva.

Rinka was inching forward, leaving the safety of darkness. Annie made a gesture to stop him, but instead she found herself following him toward the camp, towing a reluctant Baggy behind her. It seemed to her years since she had last eaten. A fantasy banquet spread before her mind's eye: braised veal, steak and kidney pie, smoked sausages, roast chicken, leg of lamb.

But Baggy stopped and would not budge. She turned on him savagely, famished, furious. And then, *what is the matter with me?*

"Rinka!"

He was poised just on the verge of the shadows, one foot raised to step into the light.

"Rinka, it's poison! To kill the survivors."

Still he hesitated, trembling with longing. As hard as it had been for her to resist, how much harder for him, who had been so hungry for so long?

"We must find Brisa," she said softly.

Rinka shook his head as if to dispel the cloud of scent. He began to sniff the ground, running a few feet in one direction, then turning back the way he had come.

"I can't find her scent. The smell from the pot overpowers

everything. But the wolves I spoke to are worried. She has been missing for three days now. Oh, what has he done to her!"

Annie did not know what to say. She hadn't expected this of Rinka, that he should love another in this way. She pitied him and also felt strangely apart from him, a little uneasy, a little left out. It was the same way she felt when she thought about Page and the king.

A light appeared inside the tent next to the apothecary's wagon. Annie could see a figure moving around, his shadow sharp on the thin burlap walls. The man set his gun on the ground and lay down beside it.

"Wait here," she whispered. From the sound of his breathing, the man was already asleep, or nearly so. She reached into her boot for the knife. With her other hand, she worked a tent stake free from the ground, glad that Gibbet's men were the kind who didn't bother to pound their stakes in well. She lay flat, cheek pressed into the ground, and lifted the loose edge of the tent. The man's face was startlingly close to her own. On his chin, whiskers poked through the skin like blades of blond grass. A hairy mole clung to his scalp.

Smirch, my old friend.

Annie took a deep breath and rolled sideways under the edge of the tent. Lightly she placed her hand on the man's chest, seeking the opening to his heavy wool jacket, and brought the knifepoint to rest where she felt his heart beating. He awoke with a start, but Annie clapped her hand over his mouth, pinching his nostrils shut with her thumb and forefinger.

"Listen."

The smell of whisky was strong in the tent, and Annie realized he had gone to sleep because he was drunk. *They're too afraid of the wolves,* she thought. Gibbet didn't plan for that.

"Where is the wolf Brisa?" Smirch shook his head. Annie pressed the knife closer to his side. He jerked away, but her knife followed him. Now he nodded. Annie uncovered his mouth, just a bit.

"Don't know name."

"The leader's mate. The leader who has been missing."

"Don't know!" he gasped.

"Think, Smirch. A wounded kinderstalk. Where are they keeping her?"

Smirch's body relaxed. "Chopper's farm."

Annie relaxed too. She knew what to do.

"Keep quiet now, Smirch, or I'll be back for you." Then she growled her very best Hippa growl in his ear.

He nodded. Sweat stood out all over his bald head.

She had the knife in his ribs. She might have given him a little stick, for Gregor. She almost did.

From her hiding place Annie watched Pip ferry buckets back and forth between the cooking pot and whatever was hidden beneath the covered wagon. A light shone dimly inside the tent, but the front of the wagon, the seat and shafts, remained in darkness.

Baggy wore a bridle but no harness or saddle. Working fast, Annie cut her petticoat into strips and tied them together into a rough sort of harness: a strip across his chest connected to another strip around his middle, behind his front legs. There was only enough petticoat left for one of the reins, so she had to cut the other one out of her cloak. The fabric was thick and full of lumps and knots. She and Rinka had fought over this part of her plan; he had insisted it would take too long. Now she felt his eyes on her, impatient.

Finally, she backed Baggy between the shafts. He stood patiently while she threaded her bootlaces through the holes in the shafts and tied them to the harness, as though he too was relieved to know what was expected of him. Impulsively, Annie dropped the frizzled waistband of her petticoat over the horse's head, decorating him for battle.

ॐ

"Girl! Knife! Kinderstalk!"

Chopper burst from one of the tents. "What is it, man? What are you saying?"

"Girl, knife!" Smirch babbled.

"What girl? What knife? Pull yourself together!"

Annie was already up in the wagon seat, the reins in her hands.

"Rinka!" she cried. "Through the middle! Of one wolf, twenty!"

Rinka burst into the light, snapping and snarling. Men screamed. The closest wolves, frenzied by hunger and the men's fear, leapt into the fray.

"Hup, Baggy! Hup, hup!"

The horse surged forward. Snow flew from beneath his hooves, and the cart, with a great groan, rolled into motion. The apothecary's tent, still tied to the wagon bed, stretched taut, then the stakes pulled free from the ground and the cloth went slack. Following Rinka's path, Baggy turned sharply and charged through camp, heading south. Annie had a brief impression of astonished faces and flailing limbs as men and wolves jumped clear of the wheels. Then they plunged back into the shadows on the other side of camp. Baggy dodged trees and rocks, jerked the wagon through ditches. Wherever Rinka led, he followed. The din of camp, the howls and cries, Chopper's staccato voice shouting orders, all began to recede except for one noise, a terrific, high-pitched shrieking that seemed instead to come closer. Annie turned in her seat. A scream caught in her throat.

The apothecary, inside the tent when it had torn free, was still clinging to the burlap, riding behind them as though on a sled. She was shrieking with rage, her child's face contorted into a fierce grimace, the black teeth bared. Her small fingers proved remarkably strong: Annie realized with horror that she was not merely hanging on, but dragging herself hand over fist across the burlap, getting closer and closer to the wagon. Her shrieks were not just random sounds, but some kind of incantation.

"*Salma, mach, minera, Scion! Salma, mach, minera, Scion! Scion, Scion, Scion!*" she shrieked, hiccupping when the tent hit a bump. She was so tiny that her body barely touched the ground as they sped along, her cloak whipping out behind her. Snow stuck to her clothes. Already she had crawled to the middle of the tent—a few more feet and she would reach the wagon bed. Her eyes were so huge and dark that Annie couldn't see any iris or pupil; it was as if she were staring through holes straight into the darkness inside the apothecary's head.

Annie snapped into action. She hadn't wanted to look at what was under the cloth, but now she took her knife from her boot and began to saw at the ties that attached the tent to the back of the wagon. Annie hewed away frantically, but her fingers felt too thick and stiff to work properly. The knife slipped and nicked one forefinger. Blood welled to the surface and Annie realized with deepening horror that she didn't feel any pain, not in her finger and not in the calf where Rinka had bitten her.

The apothecary reached the back of the wagon and began crawling across the wagon bed, still chanting her spell. Where her weight pressed into the burlap dark stains appeared. The burlap began to smoke, but the apothecary seemed immune to the poison. Her hands were not so much hands as talons, Annie saw, the skin shiny and tough.

The first tie gave way suddenly under Annie's knife. One side of the tent flapped free, flinging the apothecary nearly per-pendicular to the wagon bed. She only gripped the fabric tighter and kept crawling toward the wagon seat, chanting incessantly.

Annie could see what Gibbet had prepared for the wolves. Rabbits, or what had once been rabbits, now badly decayed. Some were little more than skeletons. Drifting through the stench of death was the tantalizing odor of the poison Pip had poured over the bodies. Annie felt her mouth water and spat vio-lently.

Her fingers had become so stiff that she could only hold the knife by pressing the handle between her palms. Panting, she gave a little cry of victory as the second tie snapped apart. But the tent did not drop off the cart. Now that the apothecary was in the wagon bed, her weight held the fabric in place. One hooked hand gripped the back of the wagon seat. The woman was close enough now that Annie could see the blue veins running beneath the pale skin of her face, the delicate mesh of capillaries covering her scalp. The terror she had felt watching the apothecary in camp overwhelmed her. *Like dark falling. Like the dark, before I could see.*

Annie pressed herself as close to the front of the wagon as she could, but still the woman reached for her. Her long nails snagged the fabric of Annie's cloak. Her smile was unmistakable now. The stiffness in Annie's hands and arms had traveled up to her shoulders. She could feel it in her calves now and her thighs, stiff as planks. In panic, Annie realized that *she* was the target of the apothecary's spell. Somehow the witch was making her immobile. If she could just get away . . . but there was nowhere to go. Her hips and torso grew rigid, as though all the blood in her body had simply stopped circulating. Annie lay nearly flat on her back now, the apothecary looming over her, a knee on her chest, the other foot still planted in the wagon bed. Annie's arms lay heavy and useless at her sides. She could still feel her feet—did her boots protect her somehow?—so Annie pushed hard with her heels, scooting across the seat. The apothecary lost her grip for a moment, startled by Annie's sudden movement. If this wagon was like Serena's, and if she was facing the right way . . . she pushed again, until her head and shoulders hung clear of the seat. From the corner of her eye she could see the ground racing away beneath them. But there it was, the wooden lever.

The apothecary stopped chanting and in the sudden quiet Annie could hear the air wheezing in and out of her own lungs. The witch pressed her knee into Annie's chest, just above her heart, so the flesh there began to stiffen. She looked into Annie's face with an expression of almost ecstatic tenderness.

"*Salma mach minera, Scion,*" she whispered. Then the apothecary shook her head and, as if Annie had spoken aloud, placed a cold finger against her lips to quiet her. Annie felt her throat tighten. Her tongue dropped into the back of her mouth.

In this last moment, using all that was left of her muscles, she managed to rock herself partway onto her side and hook her chin over the handle of the lever. Then she let herself fall back again. Her body, stiff and heavy as a corpse, bore the lever down with it. The lever slid smoothly along its track, the back of the wagon opened, and the wagon bed tipped down.

For a moment, nothing happened. The apothecary gazed at Annie with the same terrible expression of tenderness. Then, suddenly, her face changed. Baggy veered sharply to avoid a fallen tree, and part of the loose tent fabric snagged on one of its branches. Horse and wagon kept moving, but the tough burlap stretched taut, tightening like a noose around the apothecary's foot. The apothecary's body was lifted, suspended, and still she would not let go of Annie's cloak. Then came the sound of ripping fabric and the apothecary's scream as her body jerked clear of the wagon.

Sensation flooded back into Annie's limbs. Her hands flew to her breast and touched the cloth of her dress where the cloak had been torn away. Beneath her dress she could feel warm skin and the strong beating of her heart. Quickly then, she pushed the lever back into position, righting the wagon bed, but not before several of the rabbits had fallen off. The last thing Annie saw before she turned her face south was the apothecary lying facedown in a drift of burlap. Dead rabbits dotted the ground around her, each carcass surrounded by a circle of bare steaming earth where the poison burned through the snow.

Chapter 16

Rinka kept up his swift, three-legged gait, but Baggy, so full of fire at the beginning, had started to flag. They couldn't be far from the farm now. The trees had thinned out, and the tracks of men and horses showed plainly in the snow.

"Come on, Bags!" Annie urged. She heard, or imagined she heard, the clamor of Gibbet's men in the distance. Gray light filled the eastern sky. Had the night passed so quickly? Was Gibbet even now sending the first wave of wolves into battle? She turned, sickened, from the sight of the rabbits. At least they accomplished one good thing: Baggy, long since having lost interest in running toward anything, was running as hard as he could away from the smell of death.

Then, blessedly, the dark outlines of the farm buildings appeared ahead of them.

"We're here, Bags! We made it!"

Nothing about Chopper's farm had changed. The rose bushes still bloomed on either side of the farmhouse door.

The fruit trees still drooped with fruit. The lawn spread green and awful over everything.

Rinka circled the yard, nose low to the ground. His tail swung from side to side. He stopped at a circular patch of snow and started to dig.

"Brisa! Brisa! Are you there? Can you hear me? Are you badly hurt? Brisa! Brisa!"

Annie dropped to her knees beside him, scraping away handfuls of snow. There was the broad wooden disk with the iron ring at its center. Even as she tried, Annie knew she couldn't move it. Rinka barked frantically, clawing at the cover until he had raked deep furrows in the wood.

"I know she's in there. I can smell her—she's alive. Why won't she answer me?"

Annie couldn't answer him either. Was it all to end here, back at the pit, because she was still too weak to open the door? Baggy whinnied. Wolves, perhaps fifty of them, had broken through the line of trees. They flowed over the fence in a long wave.

Annie stood to meet them. She felt tall and awkward and bare, somehow. She pulled her hair forward over her shoulders.

The wolves stopped a few yards short of her. The run seemed to have cost them no effort. They regarded her intently through bright eyes.

"I am glad to see you," Annie said.

One of the wolves stepped forward. She had a short muzzle and small, almost dainty, paws. "You speak Hippa well, girl. So tell us this: where are you keeping Brisa, our queen?"

"Me? I'm not keeping her. I—"

The wolf interrupted her with a snarl. "We know you killed Rinka, and now you have his mate."

"You know this from Gibbet?" Annie said.

The wolf narrowed her eyes. Then, as suddenly as if she had been shot, she dropped to her stomach and rolled over, lifting her chin so her neck was completely exposed. Until now, Rinka had been hidden from the wolves' view by the wagon. Now he stepped from behind it, head held high. As Annie watched in amazement, the wolves dropped to the ground in one motion, offering their throats in deference to their leader. He did not immediately tell them to rise.

"Gibbet has betrayed us," Rinka said. "I made a grave error in dealing with him. We will have our revenge, but first, the queen. Rise, all of you." The wolves came up fluidly, as if one body. They were thin, terribly thin, their fur dull and matted.

The wolf who had spoken to Annie lowered her head.

"What is it, Mira?" Rinka asked.

"When Gibbet learned that the girl had taken the wagon, he sent us after her, as well as a small troop of men. Rumors passed through the camp that you were alive but we did not— of course we did not know you were with the girl."

Rinka nodded. "And the rest of the pack?"

"Two hundred already gone. He was preparing to send the rest when we left. As for men, they look so alike, it's hard to be certain. The ones he sent after us here are poor soldiers, I think, but well armed."

"Quickly, all of you. The queen."

The wolves began to dig at the hard earth around the pit. Annie watched them as if through a gauze curtain. A thousand wolves. A thousand wolves after the king, which meant a thousand wolves after Page. *Oh, please, let him not have found her.*

⁓

From a distance the men's muskets looked like a crop of sick, leafless plants. The men looked like sticks themselves, hardly better fed than the wolves. They were miners, she realized, miners from the Drop.

The wolves erupted in victorious barking. They had broken through the thawing earth to the pit beneath, the hole just wide enough for Rinka to slip through. He reappeared in a matter of seconds, dragging Brisa behind him by the scruff of the neck. Her muzzle was tied shut with a piece of cord and blood had dried around her nose and mouth. Her eyes were open but she didn't seem to recognize Rinka. Annie looked over her shoulder. The fastest men had almost reached the fence.

"Keep digging!" she cried to the wolves. Then she, too, squeezed through the opening into the pit.

Right away, she felt the darkness as a kind of relief. She could see better down here, here in the black element. The air was humid and thick, almost muddy. The pit was smaller than she remembered, too. For a moment, Annie wondered how much she'd grown in these last few months. But of course not. After she found the tunnel Gibbet must have moved the ringstone and filled in the cave, so now the dirt wall extended a few feet farther into the pit. Poor Brisa. The pit felt more like a tomb than ever. Then again, a tomb was just what Annie needed.

❧

The fence was no more than five feet high, but the first men who tried to climb over it fell back, yowling. The top bar of Chopper's fence was covered with broken glass. One man began to cut at the rope she had tied around the gate, his companions egging him on with shouts and curses.

She would have only a minute to get this done.

"Stand back!" Annie felt the wolves' many eyes on her, suspicious and interested. She coaxed Baggy backward until the rear of the wagon was even with the edge of the pit, then pushed the lever that controlled the wagon bed. At first the rabbits stuck to the wagon bed, the poison working as an adhesive. Then they began to peel free and fall. The bodies dropped by the dozens into the pit.

Rinka looked up from tending Brisa to address his pack. "This is the victory supper Gibbet promised us," he said.

With a chorus of shouts the men pushed through the gate, then stopped abruptly in the middle of the lawn. They could see now that the wolves had not attacked Annie. The aggression in their faces slackened into confusion, then fear. Mira, who seemed to have been the leader in Rinka's absence, saw her opportunity and seized it. The wolves reached the men before their muskets were even halfway to their shoulders.

A wolf dipped her head, teeth bared.

"No!" The command came not from Annie, but from

Rinka. The wolf obeyed immediately. Rinka looked at Annie as if to say, *Do whatever you plan to do, but do it quickly.*

She grabbed Baggy's bridle and ran with him to where the first man lay splayed on his back. She reached for his musket, and the wolf guarding him stepped politely aside. The man gasped. He had freckles on his forehead and the sparse beginnings of a moustache on his upper lip. For a moment his eyes locked with hers, full of fear and something else she wouldn't recognize until later: awe.

Annie moved on to each man in turn, until all the weapons were heaped in the back of the wagon. Once more, she backed Baggy up to the pit. With a clatter, the muskets slid into the hole. A muffled popping sound rose from the pit, followed by the bittersweet smell of gunpowder. She nudged a clump of dirt toward the hole with her foot and watched the darkness swallow it.

Free of her bonds, Brisa turned her head to the side and lapped frantically at the snow. Rinka hovered over her, nuzzling her head and back.

"You'd better stay with her," Annie said over her shoulder as she cut away the last of Baggy's makeshift harness.

"But you'll need help, a wolf to vouch for you."

"What about Mira?"

"Mira is . . . yes. But even so . . ." He barked an order and Mira ran over to him. The man she'd been guarding remained just as he was, thoroughly terrorized.

"Mira, go with the girl. Do as she says. She is one of us."

Annie felt her face grow hot. She kept her back turned,

pretending to fiddle with the horse, so she did not see whatever Mira did to make Rinka say, in a sharper tone, "You will do as she says."

"I will."

He approached Annie and, to her surprise, touched his muzzle to her palm. They looked at each other for a moment, Annie struggling to find words for the queer sensation around her heart.

"I'm sorry about your leg," she said.

He cocked his head to the side. "I think I got off rather easily, considering."

As she rode out of Chopper's yard, Annie turned and saw him watching her, and knew that he would watch until she disappeared among the trees of the forest.

Mira did not slow or turn around for several miles. She would run ahead, double back, run off again. Gradually the gap between her and Baggy increased, until Annie could see her only intermittently through the trees. Quite suddenly she appeared at Annie's side. She spoke in the clipped tones a parent might use with a fretful child.

"The camp is deserted. He's already sent the second wave. They'll have a good start on us already, but a pack never travels as fast as . . ." She looked doubtfully at the horse. "I hope we catch them before they reach the king's army." She started to trot away.

"Mira, wait! Rinka called Brisa queen. Is he your king?"

It seemed an innocent enough question, but the wolf's expression turned positively ferocious.

"Yes, he is our king! Some may choose not to honor him, but he is no less a king because of it."

Annie hesitated, but she was curious. "Who does not honor him?"

"Fristi and her followers. They wait for another, some figure of legend. They cannot accept the power already in our midst. She was with him the night he fought that old traitor, Sharta."

"Why do you call Sharta a traitor?"

"He abandoned his own son to serve a human. Who could forgive such an act?"

Several miles passed before Annie had the courage to speak to Mira again.

"What do you know of the apothecary?"

Mira's ears stiffened.

"The dark feeder."

"Why do you call it that?"

"That's what it does. We also call it witch, shape-changer, spell-caster. It does all of those things."

"Is she—is it an animal?"

"Human, animal. It is ancient and has many forms. And many children."

"It has *children*?"

"Why not?"

Annie decided to try a different tack. "When you say it feeds on darkness, do you mean instead of food?"

"Judging by the teeth, I'd say it eats meat. But the dark makes it strong. Light makes it weak. We have a legend that tells how the witch cast a spell to hide the moon, but that would make it very old indeed."

"Seven centuries," Annie murmured.

"In any case, I'd keep clear of it. It can't do much to you unless it can see you, and then it can do anything it wants."

Uneasily, Annie looked around her. The apothecary was everywhere and nowhere: a hand with long, dirty nails turned out to be no more than a branch full of twigs, the black tips bare of snow; the hunched shape of a shoulder nothing worse than a boulder; the glint of black teeth only the sun striking off a tree trunk slick with ice. Annie's eyes grew tired with looking. Her eyelids drooped. Baggy's rolling gait felt strangely soothing, and she found herself thinking not of the apothecary but of her own mother, and whether she had ever rocked her like this in the brief time that their lives overlapped.

"Wake up. We need to make a decision. The tracks split in two here."

"Is it part of the battle plan?" Annie struggled to remember everything she knew about warfare, which was nothing.

"I don't know."

"Which way did Gibbet go?"

Mira tossed her head. "If you can pick one man's scent out of all this, you have a better nose than I do."

Annie looked around. Hundreds of wolf tracks had turned the forest floor into a muddy slough. Tracing an individual scent would be as difficult as tracing a single set of footprints.

"Perhaps we should split up?"

Mira looked delighted.

But Annie was uneasy. Why had Gibbet split the army in two here? She peered through the trees ahead of them, but all she saw was more trees. She wished she could cut them down, just for a second, just to see.

And then she smiled, really smiled, so that Mira asked sharply, "What is it? Are you ill?"

"The cutting fields."

"Explain yourself."

"The fight will be in the cutting fields. Gibbet needs an open plain to see the battle, but he'll want the wolves hidden from view as long as possible."

"How does that explain his decision to split the pack?"

"I'm not sure." Annie closed her eyes, trying to remember. Her uncle and Chopper had approached the field separately from the east and west. She had had a clear view from where she stood . . . Her eyes flew open.

"There's a hill overlooking the fields from the north. You can climb down the wash, but it's steep and very narrow. The field is open in the other directions. They'll see the wolves coming from the west, they'll turn to fight . . . they'll turn their backs to the hill, and"—she pointed to the path branching north—"the wolves using that trail will drop down on top of them."

"Clever," Mira said.

"You take the northern branch. Like I said, the path down the hill is narrow. Block it with your body if you have to." She hesitated. "You'll be all right?"

"Certainly."

"Good-bye, then."

The wolf's expression softened, and in that moment she reminded Annie of Aunt Prim. The moment passed. Mira turned and ran swiftly along the tracks left by Gibbet's army.

The day had dawned white and cloudy and even now, at midday, the sun struggled to brighten the forest floor. For the third time in as many minutes, Baggy stopped to consider his route. Where the wolves had simply jumped clear of roots and bushes, the horse proceeded gingerly. All her coaxing, even her sharpest kicks, could not make him hurry. Abruptly, Annie turned his head straight south, and the horse, as if knowing they were headed at last to a proper road, hustled along. A quarter mile later they broke from the trees and joined the road that connected the cutting fields to Gorgetown. It was strange how quiet everything was, how normal. What had she expected, a black flag waving from every rooftop?

Two dark specks were making their way toward her, now clear against a patch of snow, now lost against the muddy ground. Wolves? They were much too small to be wolves.

Then Annie was standing in the middle of the road, the cats purring and rubbing against her ankles. Around her neck

Prudence wore a circlet of braided hair. The hair was pale gold, nearly white, without any other colors mixed in. Page's hair. Page was safe. Annie slipped the circlet onto her wrist. But Isadore wore something around his neck as well, a red ribbon shot through with gold thread, the colors of the king's army. Annie dropped the ribbon to the ground.

They were together. He had found her. She had wanted to be found.

A farmer at work in his field felt the sun's warmth on the back of his neck and straightened up, resting his spade against the toe of his boot. Nothing had grown in this plot of land for more than a decade, but every spring he turned the soil and planted seed. Lifting his face to the weak light he saw a girl fly past on a horse, her body bent nearly flat to the animal's back, her hair whipping out behind her like a black flag. What can that poor child be running from? he wondered. He watched her a moment longer, then smiled and stuck his spade into the thawing earth. She was not running away, he decided, but toward.

Chapter 17

The smells of the battlefield reached her first: death and dying, fear, of course, and exertion, clouds and clouds of doubt, and someone, somewhere, reeking of joy. She heard shouts and gunfire, the fierce barking of a wolf, cries of pain. Then they rounded a bend in the road and she reined the horse in so hard his front feet left the ground. She had wanted desperately to reach the fight, but now that she was here she wanted just as desperately to turn around and go back—not just back along the road, but back in time to the Annie who had never seen a war.

Corpses covered the field, red for the king's army, black for the wolves. The men fought with guns and swords and axes. The fighting was thickest closest to the hill, just as she had feared. The men kept their backs to the ridge. The wolves hemmed them in. Their numbers were about equal, which meant the rest of the wolves had not yet arrived. Had Mira caught up to them? Had she stopped them? Annie scanned the hilltop. There was the oak clinging by its roots to the cliff, and the spot where she had stood with Izzy and looked down at her uncle and Chopper. And there, in the shadow of the oak, a square of purple, an odd patch of color amid the landscape's grays and browns. Uncle Jock had complained for days about the purple patch on the knee of his breeches.

Womanish. I look a fool.

It's all I have. Would you rather the wind freeze your joints?

He had tipped the gun almost vertical, barrel pointing down as though he planned to fire at the very base of the wash. Of course she would be there. The king would try to protect her, might even shield her with his own body. But would he think to look up?

Look up, look up, look up.

Uncle Jock took aim, frowned, lowered his weapon, and took aim again. Page must be moving. Running back and forth, maybe looking for Annie even as Annie was looking for her.

Look up, look up, look up.

Annie watched her uncle take aim once more. He smiled. His shoulders relaxed.

She threw back her head and howled.

She left the horse—too skittish, too slow. She left her boots, useless without their laces. When she fell on the blood-slick field she got up and ran on. She climbed over the dead bodies of men and wolves. She pushed living bodies out of her way, until they seemed to move themselves, an avenue opening before her, on either side a wall of red and black. She could see them now, Page and the king, standing at the end of the avenue. They were looking at her, their mouths open in shock, in greeting.

Uncle Jock's finger moved on the trigger.

❧

Annie's body struck Page just ahead of the bullet. She felt her sister jerk in her arms, then they landed together in a heap. The king bent over them.

"Where? Where's the shooter?"

Up there, Annie tried to say, but her voice came out a snarl. The king flinched.

"Up," Annie tried again. "Uncle."

She pointed, but Uncle Jock had disappeared. The king's face turned pale.

"Look," he said to Annie. "Look."

The rest of the wolves had arrived. They crowded the hill-top. At the front stood a wolf with a reddish coat that Annie recognized from the night Sharta died. She stood stiffly, her tail held high as she surveyed the battle below. But her face . . .

She looks so sad, Annie thought. There was a stirring in the ranks behind her, a wolf pushing through to the front. Mira, foam flecking her jaws and sides heaving. Mira had reached them.

All this time Annie kept her hands pressed over her sister's throat. The bullet had struck Page in the neck, just under the jaw.

"It's only a flesh wound," she said to the king. "It's only a flesh wound," she said, again and again, as the blood ran over her hands and soaked her sister's hair.

"Is there anyone to help? Any doctor? Your Highness, answer me!"

"East," the king said. "Two sisters. A medical tent." He spoke slowly, dreamily. "Will you run there, as you ran here? I have never seen anything like it. I thought at first you were an animal."

"I'll run. Now hold your hands here, like this." Annie pressed the king's hands over her sister's wound. "Like she did for you."

"Look at them all," the king said in that same odd, dreamy tone. "Look at how they wait on you."

Annie turned, and for the first time saw what made the king speak so strangely. The battlefield had fallen perfectly still. Men and wolves seemed to have forgotten what they were doing and simply stared. On the hill above them four hundred wolves stood still and stared. They all stared at her.

Annie took a step forward. No one moved to stop her. She started to run. A white flag marked with a red cross waved at the eastern edge of the field.

A large shape stepped into her path, a wolf, rearing on its hind legs, its pelt sliding horribly from its back, a flash of white skin, whiter teeth, then a rifle butt brought down hard against her temple.

෴

Two blurred dark shapes loomed over her. Two wolves? A paw reached down, no, a hand. To help her up? Sharp pain crossed her scalp. Her hips left the ground, then her feet. She was being lifted. By the *hair*. It hurt to struggle, but she did, until the hand in her hair made a fist and jerked her head back. She found herself looking up at Gibbet's furious, blood-smeared face.

Chopper stood beside him with his rifle pointed at Annie. She saw at once why she had mistaken them for wolves. As camouflage, each wore a rough cape of wolfskin. The skins were fresh.

"What are you?" Annie said in Hippa.

Gibbet smiled. His teeth, she saw, were fake.

"This girl," he called out. "Why do you stop fighting for this girl?"

The red wolf howled her answer from the hilltop. She dropped into the wash and four hundred wolves flowed after her and through the parted ranks of soldiers. They came to a stop in front of Annie and Gibbet.

"Fristi, you wish to make trouble for me?" Gibbet snapped in Hippa.

"Release the scion," the red wolf said.

"What did you call her?"

"Release the scion."

"How do you know it's her?"

"She is the one."

"How do you *know*?" Gibbet jerked Annie's head to the side as spoke. Fristi's eyes narrowed.

"You know it as well as I. But if you need a sign—there, at the back of her neck."

Now Gibbet jerked her head forward. Fristi growled. Annie felt his finger with its sharp fingernail touch the nape of her neck where the white hair grew.

"That is nothing. A birthmark."

"A birthmark indeed. Let her go."

"Finish the fight. Then I'll give her to you. The girl, and all your land. Whatever you want."

Fristi barked high and fast. Annie recognized the order, but it wasn't Gibbet they went after. A shout of fear sounded from the top of the hill and Uncle Jock appeared from behind the oak, Mira snapping at his heels. He slashed at her with his rifle but she drove him relentlessly over the edge of the wash. Wolves waited below. He slid awkwardly down the steep hillside, trying to scramble up even as he fell. At the bottom he managed to stand and lift his gun, but there were too many, too close. Panicked, he turned and began to run, staggering through the mud. *Fool*, Annie thought. For now the wolves hunted as a pack, darting in to deliver quick, superficial bites, then backing away. They were not without cruelty. When their prey stumbled, the wolves hung back, allowing him to get to his feet before they moved in again.

"A trade?" Fristi asked.

"There is no trade," Gibbet replied. "He means nothing."

"Then he dies."

"No!" Annie cried, but her voice was lost in a volley of excited barks as the wolves brought down their prey for the final time. She was glad she could not turn her head.

"But surely this one means something?"

Wolves surrounded Chopper, snapping and snarling. Annie could smell his fear, though none showed on his face.

"No," Gibbet said. And it was true. She sensed nothing like sadness on him, no regret, no uncertainty, only his same stale odor of onions and fury.

"No more kills," Annie said.

Fristi nodded. The wolves backed away from Chopper.

"Gibbet?"

He brought her face very close to his. "What?"

She considered the wide mouth, the smile like a wound opening, the false teeth. She considered the portrait in the king's throne room, and the mine overseer six generations ago who looked so very much like this one. She considered the apothecary's spell that slowed her blood and the potion that forced flowers to bloom and men to sleep their lives away.

"I don't know what you are," she said. "But I know what made you."

"Ah, but do you know what made *you*?" He brought their faces closer still, so close that she could smell the queer, bleached bone odor of his teeth. "Do you remember your own birth? Because I remember mine."

"Let me go."

He turned her again so she faced Chopper. Chopper, whose face had never changed, who had never lowered his gun.

"What will you do now, little animal?" Gibbet whispered in her ear. "Claw me? Bite me?"

"*This*," Annie said, and brought her bare heel back as hard as she could into his shin. Gibbet yelped and doubled over. She jerked free and ran pell-mell toward the white flag.

❧

"Move aside, dear. I need to wrap her up." Serena stood over Annie and Page with a stack of clean bandages in her hands.

"She's so pale. Even her lips."

"Yes." Serena tried to smile but couldn't quite manage it. "Annie, she has lost a terrible amount of blood."

"But you closed the wound!"

"I closed it too late."

Bea took Annie's hand in hers. "We don't know that for certain, Serena."

"Bea, look at her! Already a ghost. It's wrong to give the child false hope."

"We haven't tried everything yet."

"What else? What haven't you tried?" Annie clutched Bea's hand so tightly she winced.

"There is one thing—," Beatrice began, but Serena cut her off furiously.

"I know what you're thinking, and I won't!" She turned to Annie. "Bea's mad. She means for me to do a transfusion."

"You've done it before," Bea said, "at the medical college."

"A lifetime ago! And there were a dozen doctors standing by to help."

"I'll help you," Beatrice said. Then her eyes widened.

Fristi stood inside the tent. "We await your orders, Scion."

"I have no orders for you!" Annie shouted. "Whatever you

think about me is wrong. Please, just leave me alone!" She glanced desperately at Page.

"You fear for the girl?" Fristi asked.

"My sister. Yes, I fear for her!"

"She is not your sister," the wolf said matter-of-factly. Then just as matter-of-factly, "What does she need?"

"Blood."

Fristi disappeared without another word. Annie stared after her from the tent's entrance. The battle had ended. Men and wolves searched the field for their wounded. A captain from the king's army kept guard over Chopper and Gibbet. Chopper stood stoically as ever, but Gibbet snarled something at Fristi as she ran past.

Fristi returned with a legion of wolves behind her. In their midst, looking determined and afraid, came the king.

"Miss Trewitt! The kinder . . . the wolves. I cannot understand what they want. Where is Page? Is her condition improved? What is happening?" Without waiting for an answer he pushed past her into the tent. At the sight of Page he cried out as if in pain.

"She needs blood," Beatrice said quickly, "a transfusion."

"Then you must perform one." Already the king was shrugging out of his embroidered coat and vest and unbuttoning the layers of silk underwear he wore beneath them. The scars on his face and neck where Annie had attacked him showed plainly. Beatrice and Serena gaped at him.

"Your Highness, do you mean . . . do you wish for us to operate on you?" Serena stammered.

"I do not wish it. I order it," said the king. Then he bowed once with great formality, legs straight, back flat as a table, and lay down on the blankets beside Page.

Fur grazed Annie's hand. "Scion, do not weep. Come with us."

Wolves surrounded her. They crowded the tent, pressing against Annie until she lost her balance. They caught her, as they had that night outside the palace gates, and bore her from the tent.

"Page!" Annie cried. "Page!"

But the wolves were carrying her farther and farther from the tent and the people inside it. She let her head fall back and saw two small shapes traveling through the branches above, orange and striped brown. A cry came from the tent. Or perhaps they were too far away. Perhaps it was only a bird.

At last she slept. The wolves moved gracefully beneath her, passing the burden between them without waking her.

Chapter 18

There was a draft. A very cold, persistent draft, the kind that would have Aunt Prim reciting from one of her favorite lists. *Ailments Induced as a Consequence of Malignant Breezes: Gout! Dyspepsia! Shrunken extremities! Sluggish bile!*

Annie tucked up her legs and nestled closer to the cats. If she didn't open her eyes, or listen very carefully, or smell anything, she could imagine they were back on the old straw mattress in the garret. *I had the strangest dream,* she would tell the cats, but they would lose patience halfway through and demand to be let out the window. Even now, she could feel Izzy stretch in a way that meant the warm lump of cat attached to her rib cage would soon become a fidgety cat intent on breakfast.

The floor beneath her felt cold and slightly damp. Stone. Water dripped nearby. Farther off she could hear the shushing of an underground river. The air smelled of salt and smoke and the light green, split-wood scent particular to Dour County.

Annie sat up. She was not alone. She pivoted slowly, peering in every direction. She was staring toward the back of the cave, staring toward nothing, when whiskers brushed her cheek. Then breath, hot as an oven. Annie turned her head and looked directly into the wolf's eyes. The gaze was serene, gentle even, but the animal was huge, bigger than Sharta, bigger even than Rinka. Her coat was coal black except for a diamond-shaped patch of white on the breast. Her voice sounded like the wind in the pines, whispery but strong.

"I am glad to see you awake. Welcome to Finisterre."

Annie cleared her throat to dislodge the first word, but still her voice came out a squeak.

"Where is my sister?"

"Page is well."

Annie blinked, startled. "Is she here?"

"She is with the king."

The wolf looked at Annie with a tenderness that made something in her memory groan and shift, something she had not thought of for years.

"Come with me," the wolf said. Annie followed her through a passage at the back of the cave. The space was so narrow she had to crawl on all fours to fit through. Light spilled through an opening ahead of her. The light was bright but soft, softer than sunlight.

The passage opened onto a ledge overlooking a vast, brilliant cavern. White light glowed from the vaulted ceiling and from every wall, and even from the ledge under Annie's feet. The cavern was perhaps a hundred feet across, the vault at least as high from where Annie stood and many hundreds of feet deep. All of it, every inch, was covered in white ringstone. Annie peered over the ledge. Far, far below, she could see the white walls disappear into the dark mottled surface of the sea.

"Is this the moon?" Annie asked, and blushed. It was a foolish question.

But the wolf answered her seriously. "This is how I imagine it, also. You see the roof's reflection on the water?"

Annie ran her fingers over a pattern of gashes in the stone close to where they stood. They looked like claw marks. She took the ringstone from the hem of her skirt and showed it to the wolf.

"Gibbet has been here. He gave my uncle a ringstone cut from this cave."

The wolf shook her head. "Gibbet has never been here, but you are right about the stone. Let us go make ourselves comfortable. Then I will tell you a story."

The cats were waiting for them at the front of the cave. To Annie's surprise, they greeted the wolf like an old friend. It gave her a strange feeling to see Izzy rub against the wolf's legs.

"It was you on the road to Magnifica, wasn't it?" Annie asked.

"It was. We had come to bring you home, only you turned out to be a very fast runner."

"Who are you?"

"My name is Helia. I was Sharta's mate."

"I'm sorry he died."

"I am glad you buried him. Wolves don't bury their dead, but this was fitting. Perhaps you can take me to visit his grave someday. You and Page could take me."

Annie's pulse thudded in her ears. "What do you mean?" she whispered.

The wolf sighed and lay down. She rested her chin on her crossed paws. "I'm sorry. I should be more direct. I have never had a conversation like this before." She paused. "I will start at the beginning. Do you remember the first child whose name Primrose wrote in her big book, the first child taken by the kinderstalk?"

How did this wolf know about her aunt's book? But Annie answered, because she did remember. "Phoebe Tamburlaine. But the kinderstalk didn't take her. Gibbet took all those children to work at the Drop. Their parents sold them."

"The kinderstalk did take Phoebe. We took her."

"You killed her?"

"No, but it nearly came to that. The wolves have been hungry for a long time, as long as I can remember, as long as my mother and her mother could remember. Once our territory covered all of Howland. There was plenty of game, plenty of space to roam, and then—"

"They dug the first mine. Page showed me on the map."

"Yes. So here we are squeezed into our little corner of the world, and there isn't enough room for us all, and everyone is very hungry. You can imagine the fights."

"Fights over food?"

"Over humans, mostly, and whether to hunt them for food.

Sharta and I said no, other wolves said yes." Helia gave a toothy smile. "There were times I considered it, believe me. But if we hunted humans, surely they would hunt us back? Besides, the people of Dour County had never done us any particular harm. It seemed . . . unfair." Helia looked up. "Won't you sit down?"

Annie had been standing rather stiffly, as though prepared to run at a moment's notice. She made herself sit. Prudence lay across her lap like an anchor.

Helia went on. "The child, Phoebe, was left outside after dark. What the parents intended, whether it was a mistake, I don't know. A group of us were out hunting, as usual. We caught rats around the farms. From time to time we'd find a stray chicken. But that night we found her. She was so tiny, I remember, all white and gold, like an aster.

"A wolf caught her by the ankle. I told him to let her go. He refused. We fought, and I killed him. I fled with the child.

"Sharta was furious when he learned what I had done. No wolf could excuse the killing of another wolf to protect a human child. There were so many humans and so few of us. At the time, our only thought was to run. But run where? Perhaps Sharta acted too quickly. Perhaps the pack would have let us live. I don't know.

"A witch lives in these woods, an ancient, evil thing. Sharta asked her to cast a changing spell. We thought we could hide in the form of another animal." She smiled grimly. "A fox, we thought, or a bear. Of course, she wanted payment."

"The white ringstone," Annie said.

"She asked many questions about the ringstone, how

much there was and whether it was good quality, but she refused to enter the cavern."

"What about the claw marks I saw on the wall?" Annie asked.

"That was the strangest part of all. She crouched outside the entrance with her cloak pulled tight all around her, then reached one hand in and tore a handful of stone right from the wall. When she touched the stone it seemed to hurt her, like a burn." Helia paused. "We should never have let her take the stone."

Annie wanted to put her arms around the wolf. Instead she asked, "What happened next?"

"Then she made a potion for us to drink. You can see the scar on the floor of the cave, there, where the brew bubbled over."

A patch of shiny black showed on the rock near Annie's foot. She moved her foot away.

"All four of us were to take the potion," Helia went on. "Sharta and I, our son, Rinka, and the gold child. Sharta drank. I drank. The change came over us so fast. Sharta reared up on his hind legs. His pelt fell off him as if he had been skinned alive. His beautiful face became a stranger's. I saw his horror at the sight of me.

"Rinka fled. We could not hold him. How the apothecary laughed! I still remember her words. 'To love a human child you must have a human form.' But she was wrong.

"We left the forest. We built a house and learned to farm. We could not call our older daughter, the fair one, by her real name. Instead we called her Page."

Helia tipped her head to the side. Her eyes were soft. "Soon we had another child. We named our younger daughter Annouk, an ancient name of the pack. But the name was too much for little Page to manage. She always called you Annie."

⁓ও⁓

Without Prudence on her lap, Annie wasn't sure what she would have done. Leapt to her feet and run away. Leapt into her mother's arms. Except this mother, her mother, couldn't hold her, not really.

"Why did you leave us?" She spoke the words very low, practically into the top of Prudence's head, but Helia heard her. The wolf's voice sounded tired.

"The potion wore off. You were just a baby when it happened. I returned to the pack, a wolf in a torn dress. Fristi had become a leader by then. Some of the others still wanted me punished, but she said losing my family was punishment enough."

"You lost Sharta too," Annie said. And then, slowly, the full force of it just dawning on her, "Sharta was my father."

"He was a wonderful father."

Prudence raised her head quizzically, and Annie realized she was crying and her tears were dripping all over the cat.

"When did he change back?"

"Two years after me. Perhaps he drank more of the potion than I did. Perhaps the witch did it deliberately. I don't know. He was with Jock when it happened."

"I remember. I remember the story," Annie clarified. She wished she could remember more. She wished she could remember her mother's human face.

"We watched you, you know, through the garret window. What we'd do for a glimpse of you and Page squabbling or laughing! It was Sharta's job to look after Page. I looked after you. I followed you sometimes, and your friend who was so curious about the world."

"Gregor." Tentatively, Annie leaned into the wolf's side. Her fur felt so soft. She smelled so good. "Am I what they say, the scion?"

"The prophecy of the scion is very old, handed down from mother to pup. The words may no longer mean what they once did." Helia hesitated. "Not everyone believes in prophecies as Fristi does."

"But you thought it might be me."

"Yes."

"What does the prophecy say?"

"We wrote it down for you."

Annie sat up. "You wrote it in Hippa?"

"Not in Hippa. Hippa has no letters. Did you find the page we hid in the book?"

"I couldn't read it."

"We wrote in ancient Frigic. No one could read it without the grammar." She shook her head, amused. "That first year as humans we bought everything in the bookseller's wagon. We hadn't even learned to read, but we were desperate to find something that would tell us what it meant to be human. That Frigic grammar was heavy going, to say the least, but it did prove useful."

"Page must have used it. She started to translate the prophecy."

"She was always good with letters." Helia sounded proud.

"I'm not," Annie said.

"Oh, Annouk! You have so many wonderful gifts of your own!" It was such a silly, motherly thing to say, but Annie beamed. She had a mother.

Helia bumped her gently with her head.

"Why did you go to so much trouble to hide it if you wanted me to read it?" Annie asked after a moment.

Helia sighed. "Your father and I agreed on most things, but not on what to do about the prophecy. He thought you should know it, to better prepare yourself should any need arise. I thought you should be free of old stories, and find what happiness you could in the human world. Writing in code was a sort of compromise. Besides, we didn't want anyone else to read it. Do you still have the book?"

"Yes, but it's ruined."

Helia nodded. "That's good. Better yet to burn it."

"Now tell me what the prophecy says," Annie said.

"I never wanted you to know."

"Mother—"

"Once you know, you know forever."

"Mother, tell me."

Helia spoke the words quickly, as if she didn't like the feel of them in her mouth.

"The Scion of darkness will bear the white mark,
Human form, animal heart.
Black water, radiant night,

Torn from love, wounded life.
Changeful child, shelter the pack.
Brave in battle, devour the witch."

"Devour?" Annie said.

"Let's not think about it anymore. Let's not talk. Come, the sun is out."

❧

Later, as Annie was preparing for sleep, the wolf trotted over with something in her mouth. She set it down in Annie's lap.

"I've been keeping this for you."

The red slipper had Izzy's face stitched on the toe. One of his ears was chewed. The real Izzy came over and gave the shoe a sniff. Annie ran her finger along a spray of orange thread.

"I tried many times to come for you, once it became clear the prophecy was real."

"I know."

"I sent guardians to protect you."

Annie looked at Izzy, at Prue. "I know."

"I loved you always."

❧

The last of the snow melted over the next few days. Annie found she could hardly stand to have her mother out of her sight. They walked together, ate together, slept side by side.

Fristi sent a messenger with news: the king's army was bearing its dead and injured back to Magnifica. Beatrice and Serena remained at the battlefield to care for wounded wolves. Brisa was recovering slowly. Rinka had declared the prophecy of the scion ridiculous. Fristi had declared Rinka ridiculous, apparently right to his face.

"And Page?" Annie asked. "Can I see her?"

"She will come to you. She is better now, and only waits for the king."

"Waits for the king? Why?"

"I know nothing more about it."

And what of Gibbet and his men?

Chopper, Smirch, and Pip were prisoners of the king's army. Hauler remained at large. Gibbet had begged to be transferred to the custody of the wolves, and to Annie's custody in particular.

Uncle Jock was buried where he fell in the cutting field.

Annie sat cross-legged at the entrance to the cave. She had taken the gull-rock from her dress and was tossing it from hand to hand. Helia nudged her shoulder.

"What are you thinking about, Annouk?"

Annie held the rock up to her mother's nose. "What do you smell?"

Helia sniffed. "I smell the sea. I smell you."

"But not Gregor."

"Your friend, do you think he is alive?"

Annie didn't answer. Then Helia said something that surprised her. "Why don't we look for him?"

"Can we?"

"Annouk, you have hundreds of wolves to direct as you wish."

"No!" Annie shook her head, trying to dispel the panicky feeling her mother's words caused. "Just the two of us."

"Very well. Where should we—"

"The Drop. Let's go to the Drop."

They left after dark. Helia ran along in front, sniffing out the trail, while Annie jogged behind. After several miles they stopped to rest beside a stream. Annie recognized the clearing as the place where she had seen Gibbet speak with Rinka, so many months ago. The face reflected in the stream's surface looked older than before, more serious, but also more serene. Her hair trailed in the water as she bent to drink.

"Are you ready?" Helia was clearly enjoying the hunt.

Annie looked at her feet, suddenly shy. "Can I ride on your back? The way Page did?"

"Annouk, you don't need to ride on my back. You can run alongside me."

"Please?"

"It will be faster if we run together."

Annie nodded, oddly hurt. But Helia was right—they were fast, leaping over rocks and roots, the night air streaming past cool as water. They left the forest and raced along the top of the cliff. Far below them, the dark, swollen river raced through the gorge.

❦

There was nothing left of the Drop. The tents had been pulled down, the baskets and scales packed up and carted off, the kiln behind the orphanage dismantled brick by brick. Of the orphanage itself only a jumble of charred boards remained. A notice had been tacked to one of them: "Mine closed by Royal Decree. Direct inquiries to Office of Mineral Exploration and Management, Magnifica," followed by a date and the waxy mark of a signet ring. Annie felt something brush her ankle and looked down. The cats had followed them. Izzy's orange fur was covered in soot. She stooped to brush him off, but he slipped away from her.

The doorway to the orphanage stood intact, though there were no walls on either side of it and no door left to open or close. Annie stepped through. Izzy was sitting in what had once been the middle of the floor, next to a pair of boots. They were very big boots with metal spikes fixed to the soles. The spikes had been pounded into the ground so firmly that Annie could not pull them up. The cats wreathed around the boots as if someone was standing inside them. Annie's heart beat faster. She reached into the right boot and found the vial from Grandmother Hoop that she had given to Gregor before they separated. It was empty. She reached into the left boot. At first she felt nothing, but then she found it, way down by the toe: a match.

It was a message. She knew it was a message. But what did it mean?

Gregor, Gregor, what are you trying to tell me?

And then she heard his voice, his small, tired voice, singing the answer.

Darling, what do you wish for? The dark is drawing near.

A light, Mother, a light, to find you when you're far.

"Mother! Gregor's alive! He left me a message. He knew I'd come back for him."

Helia hurried over. "What does the message say?"

"I think he's with Hauler, and he took Grandmother Hoop's medicine, and we'll find each other. No matter how far apart we are, we'll find each other."

"I am sure you will," Helia said.

She let Annie ride on her back all the way home.

Chapter 19

Annie stretched on her side and let the stone's warmth seep through her dress. Green tips of plants poked up through the dirt lapping the stones at the cave's entrance.

"It's strange how everything grows in the forest but nothing will grow on the farms," she said lazily. "Except Chopper's farm, of course."

Helia lifted her head. "You don't know?"

"Know what?"

"Dour County soil was some of the best in the country. We had such a lovely farm in the beginning. Beets, squash, potatoes, the sweetest little carrots. It was strange at first, getting used to vegetables, but I liked it. Primrose was wonderful with flowers."

"She was your friend?"

"Yes, I suppose she was."

Annie must have made a face. Helia sighed. "She wasn't always so . . . prim. Jock was a good farmer, before he met Gibbet. The four of us got on well enough. And she did keep you safe, at least at the beginning. Jock would have sold you straight to the Drop."

Annie didn't enjoy feeling beholden to Aunt Prim. "What about the soil?"

"The Drop had just opened, but at the wages Gibbet paid no one wanted to take the work. Gorgetown was a real place then, with a school and shops, not just the tavern. Merchants brought goods from the east. A man could make a decent living fishing or farming. So Gibbet paid Jock to . . . He *salted* the fields, Annouk. One by one the farms began to fail, even ours, 'for appearances,' he said. Soon Gibbet had men lining up to mine the quarry."

Annie rolled onto her back and closed her eyes to the sun. *Small greed,* she thought. The apothecary hated ringstone, but Gibbet—Gibbet loved it, loved it as another man would love his own child, simply for itself. And Gibbet not even a man, not really . . .

Helia jumped to her feet. "Annouk, they are coming!"

Serena led the horse with Page on his back. Beatrice, shadowed by her sister's body, walked beside them. They appeared and disappeared among the dark trunks, Serena's red bun glinting occasionally over the top of a bracka bush.

Annie stood. She sat down. She stood again. Bones left over from breakfast lay scattered on the ground. She kicked them into the bushes.

Baggy stepped into the clearing and the full procession came into view. Fristi carried a rope in her mouth. The rope's other end was tied around Gibbet's ankles. From time to time

Fristi stopped and jerked her head, forcing Gibbet to hobble forward. Annie saw what made the wolf impatient. Gibbet walked with a cringing, hunted posture. Every few steps he would stop and look over his shoulder, then scan the sky. Wolves stalked behind him, keeping guard, but he hardly seemed to notice them.

The horse, too, dragged something behind him—a litter, bearing a body wrapped in red and gold robes.

If only one of them would meet her eyes, it would be easier. Serena fiddled with Baggy's halter. Beatrice fiddled with the buttons on her cloak. Page fiddled with the bandage around her wrist. Only Fristi looked Annie in the face, but her eyes, calm and full of devotion, were not the ones Annie needed.

Then Prudence, who had been napping with Izzy in a patch of sunlit dirt, rose, stretched, and padded over to Beatrice.

"Oh!" Beatrice said. "Oh, Annie!"

"Dear Annie!" The next moment Annie was engulfed in Serena's familiar tea and copper scent, then passed to Bea, who smelled of beeswax and flannel, then back to Serena. They smelled of the battlefield, too, and weariness.

"Good gracious, your sister! I nearly forgot!" Serena moved to lift Page down from the horse's back but Page shooed her away. Her hair had been cropped short and stood around her head in a blonde fuzz. A white bandage covered her neck.

With a little cry she stumbled forward and dropped to her knees in front of Annie. She clung to Annie's waist. Awkwardly, Annie touched the back of her head. The shorn hair felt soft. Page was shaking. She was laughing. Her breath came in giddy bursts.

"It's just *you!*"

"Who did you expect?"

"The scion. I thought you'd be different. Serious, or hairy, or—"

Annie smiled. "Just the usual amount." She met her sister's eyes. "Why didn't you tell me Sharta was our father?"

"I wanted to, but he was afraid of what you'd think, having a beast for a father. He was afraid you'd hate him."

"He told you. You didn't hate him."

"I loved him. But he didn't tell me, and he wouldn't have."

"But you knew."

Page smiled. "It wasn't so hard to figure out. He knew which foods I hated. He knew my favorite books. And he—he was the same, even as a wolf." She studied Annie's face. "Don't feel bad you didn't recognize him. You were so young when he changed."

"I didn't remember."

"How could you?" Page said, but her eyes had focused on something past Annie's shoulder. Her face turned bright and anxious. "Hello, Mother."

The twins were whispering furiously together.

"Serena, the king—is he dead?" Annie asked.

"His heart was not strong enough to pump blood for them both," Serena said.

Annie knelt beside the king's body. His flesh was gray and had a weird rigidity to it, like a casing of clay. She felt she owed him something, some words, at least, but she didn't know what to say. She touched her palm to his chest.

"Annie, wait, he is—," Serena began, but Annie had already jumped back with a shout of surprise. Hesitantly, she reached out to touch him again. She could feel the beat of his heart.

"You said his heart failed!"

Unaccountably, Serena blushed. She looked to her sister for help. Bea smiled encouragingly. Serena cleared her throat and tried again.

"Annie—do you remember the clock I showed you the day we traveled to Magnifica together, the clock that was to be a gift for the king's bride?"

"For Page. Of course."

"Do you remember how the clock worked?"

Annie's mouth felt full of sand. "The clockwork heart? You gave him a clockwork heart?"

Serena looked at Beatrice again and the little woman stepped forward.

"She took the heart from the clock and I, well, I sewed it in. The lungs move, the heart beats, but he is not *alive*."

Serena elbowed Beatrice. "Give them to her now."

"Do you think we should?"

"Of course we should!"

Bea reached into a cloth pouch and pulled out a stack of papers bundled together with a red ribbon. "He said to give these to you if he died. He said—what were his exact words, Serena?"

" 'To please forgive a wicked king.' "

Annie looked at the stack of papers. "Dear Annie" was written at the top of the first page. She tore the ribbon away. *Dear Annie, Darling Annie, Little One, Beloved.* All of Page's letters, dozens and dozens of them.

"There are five more bundles like it," Serena said.

Annie watched the king's chest rise and fall. "Why did you do it, the metal heart?"

Bea looked over at Page, with her beautiful face and her child's haircut. "Your sister said she could not bear to live without him."

Annie looked from Page to the king, from Beatrice to Serena. She thought of Rinka pulling Brisa from the pit. She thought of Helia and Sharta worrying over the prophecy together. That strange old feeling settled in her chest, part pity, part longing, as though she knew how to love, but not quite enough. Then Izzy—Izzy, who didn't particularly like to be touched, Izzy, who hated to be held—took a few light steps and jumped into her arms. She squeezed him too tight, and he let her.

Fristi stood apart with Gibbet and his guards. Gibbet wore a gag and his hands were bound. His whole body bobbed and jerked as Annie approached.

"I won't hurt you," Annie said. "But I might lock you up."

A burst of sound came from behind the gag. Annie reached for the tie.

"Annie, is that wise?" Serena called. She stood a few yards away, uncertain whether her help was needed.

"Maybe not." Annie removed the gag.

"Lock me up! Lock me up, I beg you!"

The white false teeth formed a strange counterpoint to his stricken face, a face smooth like a child's yet indescribably old.

"You had them pulled, didn't you?" Annie said. "So you could pass for one of us."

"Please," he whispered.

"She sent you into the world. She had a purpose for you, but you failed. You fell in love with ringstone."

Gibbet's wild eyes focused on her face. "Two hundred years I looked for you, I waited for you. And yet I never really looked. What danger in a child? I thought. But I was never a child. Lock me up. Hide me. Only you can keep me safe."

His voice trailed off. A look of absolute terror crossed his face. Annie heard it too, a vibration in the air like the beating of a large bird's wings.

She would let the thing come and take what it wanted.

"Cut him loose."

Serena looked at her, stunned, but did as she was told. Barely had she cut through the ropes when Gibbet started to run. He ran wildly, first toward the cave, then veering away across the clearing.

"Mother, no! I'm sorry! Please, Mother, please, no!"

The fluttering darkness took shape and flew screaming out

of the depths of the wood. It sprang from treetop to treetop and bounded to the ground, snatching up Gibbet as though he were nothing more than a field mouse.

It had the wings and talons of a hawk, the lithe shape of a cat, the fanged human face. It was all things, and none.

"Mother, no!" Gibbet screamed as she bore him writhing into the air. Suddenly his cry changed. "Devour the witch! Devour the witch! Scion! Devour the witch!"

The apothecary turned its head and looked at Annie, just for an instant, the bright eyes full of malevolence. Then it was gone.

Silence stretched over the group for a long moment. They stared at one another, and at Annie, their leader. Gradually the normal sounds of the forest in daylight returned: the rustle of an animal burrowing into its bed of leaves, the sigh of the wind through the trees, the raven's cough, the mourning brook.

ACKNOWLEDGMENTS

My thanks to Charlotte Sheedy for wisdom; Melanie Cecka for insight; Meredith Kaffel for patience; Katharine Noel for generosity; Corinne Rocca for partnership; Elizabeth Hines and Nicholas Boggs for fellowship; Eric Puchner, Charlotte Taylor, and Katharine Breen for smarts; Cass Rogers for endurance; Jocelyn Yant for good heart; Laura Ostenso for good humor; Alison Werger for the beach; Ed Feldman for dinner; Mary Taylor Huber and Pat Hutchings for friendship; Jill Campbell for kindness; Philip Alex for guidance; the Brothers Grimm for being grim; Mr. Rorschach for his blots; the Carnegie Foundation for having my back; and my mother, Judith Puchner Breen, for everything.